DOC WILDE

AND
THE FROGS OF DOOM

TIM BYRD

G. P. Putnam's Sons

G. P. PUTNAM'S SONS
A division of Penguin Young Readers Group.
Published by The Penguin Group.
Penguin Group (USA) Inc., 375 Hudson Street, New York, NY 10014, U.S.A.
Penguin Group (Canada), 90 Eglinton Avenue East, Suite 700, Toronto, Ontario M4P 2Y3,
Canada (a division of Pearson Penguin Canada Inc.).
Penguin Books Ltd, 80 Strand, London WC2R 0RL, England.
Penguin Ireland, 25 St. Stephen's Green, Dublin 2, Ireland
(a division of Penguin Books Ltd.).
Penguin Group (Australia), 250 Camberwell Road, Camberwell, Victoria 3124, Australia
(a division of Pearson Australia Group Pty Ltd).
Penguin Books India Pvt Ltd, 11 Community Centre, Panchsheel Park,
New Delhi—110 017, India.
Penguin Group (NZ), 67 Apollo Drive, Rosedale, North Shore 0632, New Zealand
(a division of Pearson New Zealand Ltd).
Penguin Books (South Africa) (Pty) Ltd, 24 Sturdee Avenue, Rosebank,
Johannesburg 2196, South Africa.
Penguin Books Ltd, Registered Offices: 80 Strand, London WC2R 0RL, England.

Published simultaneously in Canada. Printed in the United States of America.
Design by Katrina Damkoehler. Text set in Plantin.

Library of Congress Cataloging-in-Publication Data
Byrd, Tim.
Doc Wilde and the frogs of doom / Tim Byrd.   p. cm.
Summary: Twelve-year-old Brian, ten-year-old Wren, and their father, Doc Wilde,
risk their lives in a South American rain forest as they seek the eldest member of their famous
family of adventurers, Grandpa, amidst a throng of alien frogs.
[1. Adventure and adventurers—Fiction. 2. Missing persons—Fiction. 3. Frogs—Fiction. 4.
Rain forests—South America—Fiction. 5. Extraterrestrial beings—Fiction.
6. South America—Fiction.] I. Title. PZ7.B98984Doc 2009   [Fic]—dc22   2008032493

ISBN 978-0-399-24783-5
10 9 8 7 6 5 4 3 2 1

To Nathaniel,
The *real* wild kid

Writing this book has been the literary equivalent of cooking a batch of Stone Soup; I brought some rocks, but the meat and veggies and spice came from many sources.

For inspiration, I affectionately acknowledge the spinners of countless adventure stories I've enjoyed since I was a kid, folks like Robert E. Howard, Fritz Leiber, Alexandre Dumas, Paul Dini, Karl Edward Wagner, Rafael Sabatini, Walter Gibson, Ray Harryhausen, Neil Gaiman, Joss Whedon, Norvell Page, Michael Chabon, and Robert B. Parker.

I owe a special debt to two writers from the pulp magazines of old. Lester Dent, who, under the nom de plume "Kenneth Robeson," brought the world the extravagant adventures of Doc Savage, the original superhero; and H. P. Lovecraft, whose spooky stories warned of eldritch horrors lurking just outside our world, waiting to devour it. Lovecraft's work is always readily available, and as I write this, all the Doc Savage stories are finally being reprinted in beautiful editions by Anthony Tollin's Nostalgia Ventures (www.nostalgiatown.com).

For encouragement over the years, I'd like to thank the enchanting Carmen Agra Deedy, the sensational Shane Black, and especially my noble friend Ed Hall, who never falters.

Thanks to my wonderful agent, Laura Rennert, who daily dares the frightening jungles of publishing with greater fortitude than I'll ever know. A very big thank-you to my editor Timothy Travaglini (and his right hand, Shauna Fay) for teaching me to use the scalpel and ignore the pain. Thank you for your patience; I'm a blockhead sometimes, and it can take me a while to realize when I'm wrong. This book is a much shinier diamond than it would have been without your help.

A very special thanks to comic book virtuoso Gary Chaloner, the first true friend of the Wildes. Gaz, you'll always be welcome on our adventures as far as I'm concerned.

And the biggest thank-you of all goes to my son, Nathaniel Byrd, who made me want to tell this tale in the first place.

—Tim Byrd

ONE

The Lyceum of the Wilde family's manor was a huge, odd room that seemed a combination of world-class library and Olympic gymnasium. There, Brian Wilde sat at a big oaken desk, staring at an ancient scroll till his eyes nearly crossed. An unknown work by the classical philosopher Plato, the roll of papyrus was roughly 2,500 years old. Enormously valuable, it was held with gentle precision in an airless vacuum inside a small ornate brass device. This was called, simply, a "scroll reader" and had been invented by Brian's father.

His father had also unearthed the scroll itself in a bizarre subterranean maze a mile beneath Desoto, Missouri, where it was guarded by an earth monster formed of crystalline needles as long as a man's arm. The thousand-pointed elemental creature was incredibly dangerous, but, it turned out, extremely vulnerable to high-pitched sonics, and Brian's dad had left it shattered across the stone.

As part of his daily study, Brian was translating Plato's words into English. From ancient Greek. And his Ancient Greek, though exceptional for a twelve-year-old, was pretty darned rusty.

"I could do it faster," his upside-down sister told him. Wren Wilde was hanging by her knees above him from a trapeze that swung over the desk. With each swing, her long ponytail lightly brushed the top of his head.

She was watching him. Supposedly learning from him, but actually annoying him terribly.

"No, you couldn't," he said.

"I could too."

"Vous ne pouviez pas," he said in French: *You could not.*

"Si *podria*," she said in Spanish: *I could.*

"不能," he insisted in Mandarin: *Couldn't.*

"Ninaweza," she pressed in Kiswahili: *Could.*

"Okay, smarty-pants . . . what's this word mean?"

"*Ophrys?* That's 'eyebrow.'"

"It is not."

"Is." She grinned. "Look it up."

"Hmmph." Brian reached for the translation dictionary. Surely Wren couldn't be right. Why would Plato be writing about somebody's *eyebrow*? If she was right, though, she'd never let him forget it.

He was saved from this dread possibility when the door opened, revealing Dr. Spartacus Wilde. Their dad.

"Grab your backpacks," Doc Wilde commanded.

"Your grandfather has disappeared again."

TWO

Grandpa was missing again. Cool!

As Brian powered down the scroll reader, Wren flipped from the trapeze and shot out the door. He darted after her, out of the Lyceum and up the stairs. Wren was already out of sight. She was tiny, even for a ten-year-old, but she was fast.

Reaching his bedroom, Brian dove over the half door blocking the doorway, somersaulting to his feet on the other side. This was one of the many ways the kids honed their skills: they had to do a dive roll to get in or out of their bedrooms.

Similarly, Brian's bed was thirty feet above the floor and reachable only by a difficult clamber up a climbing wall.

Brian's backpack was on his desk, ready for the field. All he needed to add was a book to read and he'd be all set.

He scanned the tightly packed shelves. *What to read, what to read . . . ?*

Into his pack went a book of Ray Bradbury dinosaur

stories. He'd already read it three times, but some books never get old.

He sprang to a small square tunnel in the wall opposite the door. Backpack hugged to his chest, he slid through the opening feetfirst.

On his back, down a slippery slide, he whirled and spiraled through spaces behind the walls, under the floors, beneath the Wilde mansion.

The slide ended abruptly and Brian flew out of a hole in the wall at the bottom into a large mat stuffed with goose down, landing like a mouse on a soft pillow.

He was in a huge chamber, bigger than a football field, carved out of solid granite 150 feet underground. Scientific equipment of all types known (and many unknown outside of the family) filled this hidden space; it was the subject of countless odd rumors, weird tales, and international legends. It was also the finest laboratory on earth: Doc Wilde's workshop.

A short distance away, Brian's dad stood before a large screen, arms across his broad chest, holding his chin in thought.

Wren had, annoyingly, gotten here before Brian and stood by their dad, mirroring his pose down to the way his fingers held his chin.

With them was Phineas Bartlett, a very thin, very stylish Englishman with a pencil-thin mustache. He was the Wildes' majordomo. A brilliant attorney and great friend, Bartlett managed the Wildes' legal matters, general itineraries, and the Wilde manor, Lyonesse, itself.

Brian slung his backpack over his shoulder and joined them.

In excited thought, the Wildes presented quite a picture. They were all long-limbed and golden: golden brown hair, golden tans, and large eyes with glittering irises that seemed composed of layered gold leaf. Brian and Wren were both a bit smaller than most kids their age, but they had reason to believe they might one day shoot to greater height, for their father stood well over six feet tall. Thousands of hours of physical training had made him muscular and agile. From the look of him, Doc Wilde might have been some ancient hero, perhaps the half-human child of a solar god, glowing with warmth and golden light.

Like the others, Brian stared at the screen.

"Is that some kind of monstro frog?" he asked.

"Yes," his father replied. His voice was deep, resonating like distant thunder.

The sinister shape on the screen was, indeed, a frog. A frog as big as a dump truck, with long, spidery claws and sharklike rows of dagger teeth.

Grandpa Wilde was in its mouth.

"Do we know where this was taken?" Wren asked.

"Or who took it?" Brian added.

Doc shook his head. "Unfortunately not."

In the photograph, Grandpa Wilde stood in the monstrous frog's gaping maw, grinning and waving at the camera. His longish white hair stuck out, looking windblown as usual. He wore rugged safari-style clothing just like Doc and the kids usually wore in their travels. In fact, he looked just like an older version of Doc himself.

The frog was actually the sculpted mouth of a cave, its stone skin mottled green with fungus and moss. All around it were brawny roots and snaking jungle vines.

Grandpa was clearly in no immediate danger when the photograph was taken. But what had happened since?

THREE

Lyonesse, Doc Wilde's manor, was immense and imposing.

Its structure was an odd mix of Gothic castle, log cabin, and Art Deco glass and steel, with an enormous white ash tree rising through its architectural core like Yggdrasil, the sacred World Tree of Norse myth. It sat on a high wooded hill eighteen miles outside the city limits of New York, a mighty guardian watching over the land.

Dr. Spartacus Wilde had designed Lyonesse and oversaw its construction. He took its name from Arthurian legend: Lyonesse was the mystic island of Sir Tristan's birth, a sunken land lost beneath the waves somewhere off the coast of Cornwall. Now this modern Lyonesse was internationally renowned as the fantastic home and headquarters of the world's greatest adventurer.

Half a mile from the hill on which the manor stood, a faint dirt track branched off the road into deep woods, ending at a well-camouflaged cave that penetrated deep into the bedrock beneath the rugged hillscape. This passage led to a spectacular underground bunker in which Doc Wilde stored his amazing assortment of vehicles.

As early evening twilight painted the hills above, an elegant jet-black automobile with three headlights zoomed from the bunker, eerily silent but for the crunch of tires on the gravelly cave floor. This muscular rocket of a car was a 1948 Tucker Torpedo. Only fifty-one of them had ever been made, and only forty-eight remained in existence. Some were in museums. Some were with wealthy collectors. They were virtually impossible to acquire.

Doc Wilde had three.

The Tucker accelerated swiftly. A titanium wall loomed in its path, but the vehicle did not slow. Seconds before impact, the wall snapped open, locking shut again after the car was through. Every hundred yards another such gate barred the way but allowed the Tucker to pass. These indestructible gates were just one of the many security measures protecting Lyonesse.

The unusual automobile shot from the cave onto the dirt track through the forest.

Doc Wilde had made some modifications to the three Tucker Torpedoes so they would be truly adventure-worthy. Their steel bodies were reinforced with a spray-on armor coating, the windows were unbreakable glass, and the tires were made of rupture-proof polymer gels. The old gasoline engines were replaced with solar/hydrogen engines of Doc's own invention, eliminating all polluting emissions. And running boards had been added along the sides.

When the weather was nice (and sometimes when it wasn't), Doc liked to ride outside the car on the running board. In times of emergency, this served the additional purpose of making Doc visible to law enforcement officials, who knew that if Doc Wilde was breaking traffic laws, it had to be for a very good reason, so they would try to clear the way and offer any assistance he might require.

The weather was nice now, and Doc was out on the driver's-side running board, the wind blasting through his hair, his mighty arms holding tight. He wore a white safari shirt with epaulets on the shoulders, khaki cargo pants, and leather boots. Over his shirt he wore his field vest, brown and full of pockets holding numerous useful tools and gizmos he always took with him on his travels.

Brian and Wren rode in the Tucker's backseat, wearing clothes identical to their dad's. The Wildes called these outfits their "danger clothes."

Behind the wheel was Doc's driver and pilot, an Irishman named Declan mac Coul. Declan's hair and beard were shaggy red, and while he was just a few inches taller than five feet, he weighed as much as Doc. He was like a short bear and all muscle. There were many mysteries about Declan mac Coul, but one thing they knew for sure was that he could always be counted on completely.

Next to Declan sat Phineas Bartlett in a dapper suit and derby hat, holding a cane with an ornate eagle's head handle of purest silver.

Spraying dust, the Tucker veered from the dirt track onto the main road into town. Bartlett scowled at Declan. "Slow down now, you misbegotten ape."

"Funny you callin' me an ape, all natty in that monkey suit," Declan replied. But he did slow to the speed limit, as they were no longer on Doc's private land.

When Declan and Bartlett addressed each other, the two men's voices oozed disgust and dislike. But actually, they were the greatest of friends.

Wren interrupted their sparring. "Declan? Bartlett? Do either of you know what *ophrys* means?"

Brian shot her a look. The little trickster hadn't forgotten their squabble.

Bartlett chuckled. "You'll need to wait till Declan learns *English* before you start tormenting him with Ancient Greek. But *ophrys* means 'eyebrow,' if I recall correctly," which he did. Phineas Bartlett recalled *every-*

thing correctly; he had an eidetic memory (often called a "photographic memory") and had total recall of everything he'd ever read.

Wren grinned at her big brother. "Gotcha."

Declan snorted. "You *would* know that."

Bartlett smiled. "The benefits of a high*brow* education."

Wren grinned at Brian even more. He scowled and tried to ignore her.

Bartlett gazed benignly at Declan. "Aristotle tells us, 'Educated men are as much superior to uneducated men as the living are to the dead.'"

Bartlett was familiar with lots of quotations.

"Well," Declan said, "I reckon that means I'm superior to Aristotle, me bein' alive and him bein' dead. So why should I listen to him?"

"Where's Dad?!?"

Wren suddenly cried. Startled, everyone glanced out the windows.

Doc Wilde was no longer on the running board.

FOUR

Declan slammed on the brakes, the Tucker's tires skidding asphalt in a long screech. *"DOC?"* he shouted out the open window.

There was no reply.

He and Bartlett unsnapped their seat belts and sprang from the car, scanning the empty gloom behind them. Wren and Brian scrambled out the rear doors.

"I don't see him," Brian said. His heart pounding, he clawed at a pocket on his vest and pulled out his communicator.

"Dad?!?" he shouted into it. "Dad, are you there? *Dad?!?"*

His father did not reply. **Where was he?**

"Get in the car," Declan mac Coul ordered. "We'll go back and find him."

Everyone jumped back into their seats, slamming doors.

"Kids?" Doc Wilde's voice boomed from Brian's communicator. Relief washed through them.

Bartlett and Declan whirled to face Brian as he responded.

"Dad! Where are you?"

His father's voice replied: "I'm about a mile back along the road."

Wren had her communicator out too. "Are you okay?" she asked.

"Yes," Doc Wilde answered. "Sorry I couldn't answer earlier. Come back, swiftly. I'll tell you what happened when we're together again. But be alert, there's danger afoot."

Declan spun the Tucker Torpedo and rocketed back the way they had come. Soon, the beams of the car's three headlamps washed over Dr. Spartacus Wilde, who stood on the right side of the road. He raised his hand in a wave, his golden eyes glittering as they caught the light.

He was unharmed, though the right sleeve of his shirt had been ripped. It hung raggedly between his shoulder and the cuff still around his wrist, revealing the sleek muscles of his arm.

Everyone scrambled from the car and gathered before him.

"What happened, Dad?" Brian asked.

FIVE

A few minutes ago: Doc Wilde grinned, the brisk wash of wind around the Tucker smoothing his hair back so that it looked like a golden skullcap. His clothes rippled in the wind, his muscles bulging as he held on.

Through Declan's open window, Doc could hear the muted sounds of conversation, though the words were unclear. From the sharpness in Declan and Bartlett's voices, he judged they were arguing. But then, if those two were within speaking distance, they were usually bedeviling each other.

The twilight was fading from navy blue to black as night fell. Trees along the roadside swayed gently in a breeze. The car was so quiet and his hearing so keen that even with the wind from the Tucker's speed roaring around him, he could hear crickets and frogs singing their evening songs.

Ahead, to the right, something moved in the shadows among the trees. Doc tried to make it out, but the

Tucker reached the spot quickly. As he stared across the car's roof into the shadows, one shadow detached itself and leaped over the car, so fast it took him off guard, which was not an easy thing to do.

The dark shape crashed into him, clutching at his shoulders, its weight knocking him from the running board. Doc's body was still traveling at sixty-five miles per hour as he fell toward the hard asphalt.

In midfall, Doc Wilde grabbed the shape with one hand, wrenching its mass off him. He felt its hand (or claw?) grasp and rip his sleeve as it fell away in a different direction.

Doc tucked his chin and pulled himself into a tight ball, shifting his weight a fraction of a second before impact so that he'd strike the ground at a better angle. He hit the road in a ball, spinning madly, and rolled as smoothly as it is possible for a human to roll under such conditions.

As the Tucker sped away, Doc's roll ended in the grass by the roadside. As he stood, his head reeled with brain-racking dizziness. Using a mind technique learned from a ninja monk in northern Japan who would somersault for miles down forested mountainsides, Doc cleared his senses. He dropped into a defensive stance and looked for his attacker.

About forty feet back was a shadowy lump in the grass. Staggering, it heaved itself to its feet. Doc's eyes couldn't make out its exact shape, and he realized it was wearing a cloak or loose robe.

He charged it just as he heard Brian's voice come over his communicator.

The shape turned toward him, then leaped into the woods. The leap carried it at least thirty feet. Doc tried to catch up, but the shape leaped again into the darkness, then again, and it was gone.

All Doc had seen was the dark shapelessness of its cloaked form and, when it looked at him, *huge bulging round yellow eyes* . . .

SIX

"How big *were* its eyes, Dad?" Wren asked.

"Roughly the size of baseballs. The thing wasn't human, at least not of the everyday variety."

"Do you think this has anything to do with Grandpa?" Brian asked. He stared out into the woods, watching for motion. Was the thing still lurking out there, watching, perhaps waiting to try again? Perhaps not alone?

"We can't be certain," Doc Wilde said. "But it seems likely."

Brian had a thought. "Were its eyes *frog*like, Dad?"

Doc Wilde smiled and nodded. "Yes, they were."

Brian grinned back.

"Froglike?" Declan said. "Ah, like the frog cave in the picture!"

The group returned to the Tucker Torpedo. Doc popped the trunk and grabbed an unshredded shirt. He always kept spares handy; no matter how well made they might be, his shirts inevitably wound up ripped. As the others got into the car, Doc hopped back on the running board, seemingly unconcerned about the possibility of another attack. Maybe even excited at the prospect.

Declan turned the car back toward town, and off they went. They had a very important appointment to keep.

They hoped they'd make it in time.

SEVEN

"You're five minutes late," Grandma Pat said when they arrived. "But I love you anyway."

She smiled warmly and motioned them to enter. As they filed past, she greeted her son and grandkids with kisses and let Declan mac Coul and Phineas Bartlett kiss her hand.

Patricia Wilde was a beautiful woman with the wit and vim of a 1940s movie star, which, in fact, she had been. She was shapely and nearly six feet tall, ever exquisitely dressed, with shining golden brown eyes and long bronze hair streaked slightly with white. The kids had always been very close to both their grandparents but had grown even closer to their grandmother in the years since their mother had died.

The vast condominium in which Grandma and Grandpa Wilde lived filled the entire eighty-sixth floor of the tallest, most elegant building in New York City, the Empire State Building. Grandpa Wilde had lived there since the 1930s, before he and Grandma had even been a couple.

They followed her past invaluable artifacts, exquisite paintings, pristine tapestries, pagan statues, fossilized bones, and master weaponry. The furniture was antique and wooden and looked like it belonged in a nineteenth-century gentlemen's club. And there were books everywhere. Shelves and shelves of books, books in towering stacks, books on tables. Like Doc and the kids, the grandparents Wilde liked only one thing more than adventuring: reading.

Grandma Pat led them to the dining room, where they all took their places around a large oaken table of Camelot-esque roundness.

"We don't have you over for dinner often, so I whipped up your favorite," she told Doc.

He smiled. "Thanks, Mom."

Brian and Wren spoke together: "Yes, thank you, Grandma!"

In the middle of the table was a large basket full of crispy fried chicken, with sides of corn on the cob and garlic rice with Tasmanian truffles. Everyone dug in hungrily.

"I got your e-mail with the photo of Dad in the frog

cave," Doc told his mother. "Do you know where the cave is?"

She shook her head. "You know how he is. He goes off somewhere to do research or see a friend, and the next thing you know, he's battling evil in some odd corner of the world. This time he went to Boston to give a speech at Harvard. That was about a month ago. I've been abroad myself, and hadn't heard a thing from him until I returned this morning to find that his plane had come home empty on autoreturn. There was a packet inside."

"Was it the photograph?" Brian asked.

"Yes. But that wasn't all." She left the room, quickly returning and placing an item on the table by Doc's plate.

"This was in the packet too."

They all stared, but it was Wren who spoke first.

"Wow . . ."

EIGHT

It was a frog, carved from solid emerald, with tiny bloodred rubies for eyes.

Brian hefted it in his palm. It was heavy, with the same gaping mouth, shark teeth, and spidery claws as the sculptured cave mouth in the picture.

He passed it to Wren. "Cool frog," she said. "It must be worth a million dollars."

"Likely more," Grandma Pat said.

Declan whistled in appreciation. "Aye, it's a beauty . . . or at least as much a beauty as a hideous monster frog can be. Doc, is this thing familiar to you at all? Know any demon frogs of legend or anything?"

"Nothing like this."

"Perhaps it's a *real* creature," Wren said.

Doc smiled. "Intriguing thought." He turned to his

mother. "We'll stay the night and head for Boston in the morning to pick up Dad's trail."

"Uh, Dad . . . ?" Wren started.

Everyone looked at her.

"What are those creepy things crawling on the window?"

NINE

The Wildes moved to the large window. The view from the eighty-sixth floor was spectacular, looking out over the city lights for miles. On a clear day, you could see into four other states. A block away and a few floors down, a police blimp drifted like a bubble in the ocean of night. Far below, over a quarter of a mile down, streams of light from thousands of headlights marked street level.

The view now was unusual, however, because it was obscured by fist-sized lumps oozing around on the outside surface of the glass. Lumps with bulbous round eyes.

Frogs.

There were at least a dozen of them, and they were the ugliest frogs any of them had ever seen. Their skins were yellowish, with scabby-looking patches of black warts. Where they had no warts, their flesh quivered roughly in the wind.

Brian looked at the feet for claws, wondering if these

were the monster frogs that inspired the cave in the photo, but they didn't appear to be. Their stubby toes had suction cups, and their feet were like yellowish wads of chewed gum that squished securely to the glass and left wet smears when pulled away.

They didn't look dangerous, but they did look gross.

As the humans stood near the glass, the frogs pulled their bloated forms toward them, their bulging eyes shifting, focusing . . . trying to get a better look at the people inside!

"I'm thinkin' these fellas are connected to this other business," Declan said with a chuckle.

"I was thinking they were relatives of yours," Bartlett said, "then I realized they're many rungs ahead of you on the evolutionary ladder."

"Well, it *would* look that way to *you*," Declan replied, "way down there at the foot of the ladder."

"We need one to examine," Doc said. "Let's go."

The others looked at Doc, then back out the window at the frogs and the eighty-six-floor drop to the streets below.

Brian's eyes were wide.

"We're going out *there?*"

TEN

The Wilde condominium perched 1,050 feet
above the street. From the eighty-sixth floor, it already
provided an eagle's view of the city, but above it the
building climbed another sixteen stories, reaching 1,224
feet.

A long way to fall.

At the top of the building, a 230-foot-high dirigible
mast pierced the sky, a towering pole used as a tethering
point for the great airships. At the base of the mast was
a passenger platform that also served as an observation
deck for tourists.

The rooftop elevator opened and Dr. Spartacus
Wilde strode out, followed by his kids, his aides, and
Grandma Pat.

There were some tourists milling about, oohing and
aahing over the wondrous metropolis, talking about how
the people below looked like ants (even though it was
night and they couldn't actually see any people). They

were captivated to be on the top of the world. Or as near to it as they'd ever get, anyway.

(Doc and his kids had been to the actual top of the world, a spot unknown to all but a handful of people, higher than Everest and more dangerous than a bathtub full of black widows. But that's a tale for a different time . . .)

At the sight of the world-famous Wildes, most of the visitors instantly decided this vacation was their best ever and started mentally rehearsing the anecdote for folks back home. Little did they realize their anecdote would get even better.

Without a word, the intrepid crew moved to the edge of the platform. To the tourists' amazement, Doc Wilde lifted his twelve-year-old son and threw him over the high railing. Brian plummeted from sight.

A gasp burst from every observer. Phineas Bartlett raised one eyebrow and cocked a look at Declan mac Coul. The two men separated to walk among the shocked tourists, calming their fears.

Already out of sight of anyone inside the railing, Brian had everything under control. In fact, he and his sister had argued over who'd get to perform this task, and it was his turn.

His fall slowed with a slight springiness about thirty feet below the platform, and he swung at the end of a hair-thin titanium-alloy jumpline that was hooked into his belt buckle.

The wire was strong enough to support an elephant but elastic enough to stretch and gently slow his fall without snapping him back up as a bungee cord would. Above, it looped around one of the platform rails, with its far end locked into his father's belt.

All the same, Brian's stomach dropped as he looked down, down, down at nothing for over a thousand feet. If he fell, he'd fall for nearly a minute before splatting like a water balloon on the avenue below.

He loved being a Wilde. He really did. And he *had* nearly wrestled his little sister to get to do this. But sometimes, like at that *very* second, he briefly questioned the craziness of his life. Sometimes, he thought insanity ran in his family's genes.

He had voiced that thought to Phineas Bartlett once and been rewarded with one of the Englishman's quotations: "Brian, just remember what Virgil wrote: *'Audentes fortuna iuvat.'*"

Fortune favors the brave. That could have been the Wilde family motto, and they each proved it personally at least five or ten times a week.

"You okay, Brian?" his dad's voice asked from the plug in his ear.

"Couldn't be better," Brian said into the communicator in the collar of his vest.

"Good. I'll start lowering you. Let me know when you near the frogs."

"Okay."

Frogs. He was hanging from the tallest skyscraper in the city on a wire he could barely see so he could grab a couple of giant, butt-ugly, gooshy frogs off a window. And for all he knew, these things might have teeth like the monster frog statuette. He had a sudden image of the bunch of them jumping onto him with their gummy bellies and sucking toes, toothy mouths ripping . . .

The jumpline reeled out, and Brian dropped fast. He put the image out of his head. He had on thick gloves and goggles anyway, just in case.

Down he went . . .

The wind was strong, spinning him and swinging him into the building.

He was enjoying himself. This reminded him of some of the exercises he practiced in the Lyceum at home, and that put the whole activity in its proper light. This was *adventure*. It was what he did.

He kicked the wall and flipped over so that he was dropping headfirst, staring down the endless wall, zipping groundward in a bullet dive. He started to laugh.

Yes, he loved being a Wilde.

He could see the lumps slimed to the big window of his grandparents' condo.

"I'm close," he said into his communicator.

The unreeling of the wire slowed, checking his fall. By the eighty-seventh floor, he was descending at a far gentler pace.

"I'm here," he announced as he reached the eighty-sixth floor.

The jumpline stopped. Brian flipped right-side up. He could see into the condo's dining room, where their food was waiting patiently.

The frogs were just as wretched out here as they'd seemed from inside, like tree frogs living near a nuclear reactor. They slowly shifted their sticky bulks, rolling their bulging eyes till they were staring right at him. *Aware* of him. *Interested* in him.

And, suddenly, **SWARMING** toward him.

ELEVEN

The frogs closed in.

They couldn't reach Brian where he hung on the jumpline unless they hopped (assuming they *could* hop or hop enough to reach him and not just plummet straight to the street). But they oozed into the area of the window directly in front of him.

Brian smiled at their attempted aggression. He hadn't a clue how they'd gotten up here or what kind of threat, if any, they could possibly pose, but they were as funny as they were disgusting.

He'd still need to be careful, though. There was still that possibility of sharp teeth or poison in their skin or mouths or even sprayed from weird glands.

"Dad," Brian said into his communicator, "the frogs are trying to get me. They can't, but it's clear they want to."

"Stay alert," Doc's voice responded. "If my suspicions about these things are correct, they probably don't pose much actual threat, but I'm hypothesizing on very limited information."

"Right." He wanted to ask what those suspicions were but knew his father wouldn't go into it now. He would want Brian's mind focused entirely on what he was doing.

crrroak.

As it neared him, one of the frogs belched out the loudest croak he'd ever heard. The others immediately joined in: **crrroak! CROAK! CRRRROAKKK!**

It was obnoxious and unnerving, but it did have one benefit: he could see into their mouths, and he saw no sharp teeth.

He was supposed to bring back two: one for observation, and an extra for dissection if it seemed necessary. He braced both feet against the glass. The frogs charged him in extreme slow motion. One hand steady on the wire, Brian reached the other toward a frog.

As he neared, the thing's eyes nearly crossed trying to keep his hand in sight. Brian's fingers closed over the creature. Even through his glove, he felt his fingertips slip in the mucus of its skin. He gingerly closed his grip, feeling its body squeeze like a blob of very soft rubber.

CROAK! The thing yelled at him.

"Yeah, yeah, yeah," he muttered. He pulled at it, trying to unstick it from the glass, but it was like pulling at a huge wad of taffy.

He let go of the jumpline with his other hand and leaned in to dig his fingers under the frog's gummy belly, trying to pry it while pulling with the first hand.

Yuck.

CROAK-CRRROAK-CRRRRRROOOOAK!

The frog wasn't enjoying this any more than Brian was. And it wasn't budging from the window.

Brian grinned at a sudden thought. Digging in his vest, he pulled out his emergency repair kit, taking from it a titanium sewing needle. Holding the creature with one hand, he jabbed its slimy little frog bottom with the needle.

CAAAARRRROOOOAKkk!

The frog's eyes bulged bigger, its body heaving in Brian's grip. It tried to jump, which separated its belly from the glass, just enough so that Brian could pull it off the window.

With the frog squirming in his hand, Brian spun, trying to regain his equilibrium. The chorus of croaks swelled louder, the frogs agitated by his floundering. His heart pounding, Brian hung loosely to let the line stabilize.

The frog was stuck to his fingers, its gummy belly adhered to the leather of his glove. Brian raised the hand toward his face, nearly eye to eye with the frog.

Crroak, the frog said.

"Croak," he said back, and stuffed the frog into a large pouch slung at his hip. He shook his hand roughly, trying to dislodge the sticky creature, but it stayed stuck till another poke from the needle convinced it to let go.

Using the needle, Brian got the second specimen easily. He was about to poke it again to get it in the bag with its buddy when he felt a quiver in the line from which he hung. He looked up.

"Oh no," Brian muttered. A man-size shape hunched directly above him, about twenty feet up. It crouched on the wall, facing down, staring at him with bulging, baseball-size yellow eyes.

"Dad, I'm in trouble!"

Brian shouted into his communicator, even as he realized the thing was doing something to the jumpline.

The wire broke.

With a frightened cry, Brian fell.

TWELVE

"Brian, what is it?" Doc Wilde shouted into his communicator.

The jump line between him and Brian slackened. Doc leaped up the vertical bars of the railing. Wren charged the railing too, desperate to see what was happening to her brother. Behind her, a tourist screamed, and she saw something hurling toward her father as he climbed.

"DAD!" Wren shouted in warning.

The thing slammed into Doc, knocking him from the bars. He hit the ground in a roll, smoothly coming to his feet to face his attacker.

Or, to be more precise, *ATTACKERS.*

They were five creatures like the one that had attacked Doc earlier on the car, only now they were close enough for him to have a good look. As expected, the creatures were rather froggish in appearance.

They wore dark green hooded robes that hid most of their bodies, but they were clearly the size of men and humanoid in shape. All their visible skin was mottled green and moist like amphibian skin. Their hands extended from floppy sleeves and had long clawed fingers with thin webs between them, and their feet occasionally slipped from beneath their robes, resembling rubbery scuba fins. Their faces were dominated by their bulging round eyes and distinctly frog-like snouts. Their mouths gaped, revealing sharp teeth like those Brian had feared the frogs on the window might possess.

As the man-frogs came at the Wildes, the tourists around them shrieked and ran in a slapstick scramble for cover or escape.

Doc gritted his teeth in intense and uncharacteristic anger. This thing was keeping him from his son.

The man-frog facing him crouched slightly, warning Doc of the leap that instantly followed. Doc dodged, and the creature shot past him into the railing, landing in a sideways crouch on the bars with the grace of a squirrel. It leaped at him again so fast that this time Doc couldn't dodge. They grappled, its claws tearing his shirt to get at the skin and muscle beneath.

A few yards away, the claws of a man-frog swiped at Wren as she darted about its feet. She grabbed the hem of its robe, twisting it around the beast's legs and toppling it to the ground.

Phineas Bartlett twisted the silver eagle's head handle of his cane, drawing from the cane's shaft a thin sword with which he jabbed and slashed to keep the things at bay.

Grandma Pat used an aikido move to heave an attacker into the railing, but it kicked off the rails and leaped right back at her. Nearby, Declan and a man-frog thrashed on the floor in a muscle-straining wrestling match.

And during it all, Brian plummeted toward the street FAR, FAR BELOW . . .

THIRTEEN

It would be reassuring to learn that Brian had a special parachute in the back of his vest, or that he had a grappling hook with which to snag a passing ledge, or that his acrobatic training allowed him to grab a flagpole and spin around it like a comic book superhero to save himself.

But none of that was true.

So, while a battle raged far above him, Brian Wilde fell from his broken line, screaming all the way.

The man-frog crouching on the wall above him made a long croaking noise that might have been a chuckle. Then it turned and lizard-climbed toward the top of the building.

A minute ago, Brian had the thought that someone falling from this building would take *almost a minute* to reach the ground, meaning it was an incredibly long fall (which it was).

Now, though, as he fell, Brian's thought was that he had *less than a minute* before hitting the ground. Meaning that while it *was* an incredibly long fall, it really wasn't that long a time if it was to be the rest of your life.

As the adventuring son of Dr. Spartacus Wilde, Brian had an unusually swift reaction time in dangerous circumstances, and he reacted just seconds after the jumpline broke. He knew that there was really no rational way he could survive this predicament, so he went with an option that was simply insane.

The second frog was still stuck to his hand. He reached his other hand into his pouch and grabbed the first. He twisted the squishy thing in his grip, getting that hand's fingers caught on the frog's gooey belly. Now he had a frog stuck to each hand.

Then Brian did the only thing he could think of to save his life. He slapped both frogs against the side of the building that was rushing past as he fell, gripping them as tightly as he could to keep from being jerked loose.

Amazingly, the frogs stuck to the wall! His weight and speed pulled them down, smearing the building with their gluey goo, but their drag against the wall actually slowed his fall, finally stopping it altogether.

Brian hung from the frogs like they were handles, still many hundreds of feet above the street.

"Wow, it worked," Brian said, his voice remarkably calm. "Now what?"

FOURTEEN

Atop the building, the battle raged on. Numerically, the sides were evenly matched, five versus five. But when it came to ability, the amphibious side was far outclassed, and in short order the fight shifted in the heroes' favor.

An enormous **CROAK!** boomed from above, and everyone looked up to see a small blimp hovering near the tip of the dirigible mast. It was the police blimp they'd seen earlier through Grandma Pat's window, but several man-shaped figures clambered excitedly on its balloon. At the moment, the craft was clearly not crewed by lawmen.

The man-frog that cut Brian's jumpline bounded up from the side of the building, pausing in a crouch atop the railing. It cast its bulging gaze around the platform, opened its toothy mouth and shouted, *"MMMRRRRRIIIBBBIT!"* Then it leaped from the rail to the bottom of the mast (a good fifty feet away!) and started to climb.

As a second **CROAK!** boomed down from the blimp, the other man-frogs followed its lead, breaking from their battles and jumping to the mast.

"After them!"

Doc shouted. "Try to capture at least one!"

Wren glanced back just as her dad dived after Brian like he was diving into a pool, shooting out of sight. Despite his command, she turned from the chase and ran back to the rail, scared for her brother and now for her father as well.

The rest of Doc's team charged the dirigible mast.

The man-frogs, though, were *fast*. They surged up the mast pole in short hops, reaching its tip and leaping one by one to the blimp, sticking to its sides. When all were aboard, the blimp's engines hummed and it swung away and drifted into the night.

FIFTEEN

By the time Doc Wilde dropped down on his own jumpline to help his son, the frogs that Brian had used to save his life were too squeezed and smeared to be of much use as specimens. Before rising back to the 102nd-floor platform, though, Brian and his father pried three more off the elder Wildes' windows. These three kept up their croaking in Brian's pouch all the way to Grandpa Wilde's huge laboratory in the condominium.

After calling the police to report the attack and learning that the police were indeed missing a blimp, Grandma Pat accompanied Declan mac Coul and Phineas Bartlett back to the dining room. There, the two men honored her by restraining themselves from their usual duel of insults.

In the lab, Wren and Brian hovered by their father as he examined the bizarre frogs.

"Do you recognize this species?" Doc asked his kids.

Brian and Wren—who were well trained in zoology—

both shook their heads. "It doesn't look like any known species that I can remember," Brian said.

"You're right," Doc said. "It's not anything known. That means it's either previously undiscovered, a mutated offshoot of some other species, an artificially created hybrid, or something truly alien or supernatural."

"You mean it might be from another planet or dimension?" Wren asked.

"It could be. I'm leaving that theory for last, however, until we've exhausted all the more-earthly possibilities."

They nodded. Their father was very much a man of science and preferred problems he could solve rationally via the scientific method. All the same, he kept an open mind and pursued any challenge with passion no matter how illogical or arcane.

Doc prodded and probed the frogs awhile, testing their responses, analyzing their biological makeup. The creatures made annoyed croaks and kept their eyes on him the whole time, never even glancing away.

"I think my hunch was correct," he said finally. "But we need to dissect one to make certain."

They stored two of the frogs in a small cage, and the amphibians watched through the bars as Doc gently gassed the third and prepared it for dissection. Then he turned the actual operation over to the kids while he observed and gave them pointers.

Fifteen minutes later, the dissection was complete.

"It's just as I suspected," Doc said, pointing into the frog. "They have an unusually complex nervous system centering on this small organ just behind the brain. I think that organ is a psychic antenna."

"They read minds?" Brian asked. This was getting more interesting all the time.

Doc smiled but shook his head. "No. They're not *that* smart. You've noticed how they won't let us out of their sight? I think it's because that's their job. They're here to keep an eye on us."

"*Spy* frogs?" Wren asked, amazed.

"Yes, spy frogs. Everything our little friends see and hear goes into that antenna organ, then is psychically broadcast to someone or something that can read their signals."

He leaned close to the cage, looking the frogs in the eye. "You're watching us right now, aren't you? Care to tell us what you're up to?"

The frogs stared.

"I didn't think so."

The Wildes peeled off their latex gloves and lab coats,

then washed up in the sink with plenty of soap and hot water.

"What about those robed frog guys?" Brian asked. "What are they? Are they the guys receiving the signals?"

"Maybe," Doc answered, "though I suspect they're just soldiers. Either way, it's clear someone doesn't want us involved in whatever it is they're up to."

SIXTEEN

Early the next morning, an autogyro shot from New York to Massachusetts, silent as a falling leaf.

An autogyro is a hybrid of a small plane and a helicopter but is far more maneuverable than either, being able to take off and land straight up and down, veer into amazing turns that would scare an airplane pilot silly, and make pinpoint landings. This one was also capable of reaching amazingly high speeds in flight.

While autogyros have been around almost as long as airplanes, this particular vehicle was designed and hand-built by Dr. Spartacus Wilde. He'd named it *Colibri*, which means "hummingbird" in French. It was the swiftest, most stable light aircraft ever built.

Declan mac Coul piloted the autogyro into the airspace just above Boston, navigating both by sight and GPS. He swooped in over Cambridge, to Harvard University, landing gently in Harvard Yard. Several dozen passing students watched the craft with wonder, as though it were a flying saucer.

The *Colibri*'s hatch opened, and Doc Wilde strode out, golden in the morning sun. All the students recognized him immediately and smiled at their good fortune to see a living legend, one of the greatest scientists and adventurers who ever lived. Brian and Wren followed, then Phineas Bartlett stepped elegantly onto the grass, cane in hand.

Leaving Declan to watch the autogyro, they crossed the Yard, went a short distance up Concord Avenue, and made their way to 60 Garden Street, the Harvard-Smithsonian Center for Astrophysics, also known as the "CfA."

Once inside, they were shown to a meeting room, and a minute later a tall black man in jeans and a long-sleeved shirt entered.

"Dr. Wilde!" he said. "It's a pleasure to meet you. I'm Nolan Haines, the director here."

Doc shook the scientist's hand and introduced him to Bartlett and the kids. "Dr. Haines, the pleasure is mine. I'm an admirer of your work."

"Please, have a seat," Dr. Haines told them, and they took places at the meeting table. "Now, what can I do for you?"

"I understand my father spoke here a few weeks ago. He has since disappeared, and we're trying to trace his movements."

"Oh my, I'm sorry to hear that. I quite like your father."

"He was speaking about dark matter, correct?"

Nolan Haines nodded. "Yes, that's right."

"Excuse me," Wren said, "but what *is* dark matter? We haven't reached astrophysics in our studies yet."

Haines smiled. "Well, dear, I'd say you have plenty of time to get to it." He paused, collecting his thoughts. "Dark matter . . . are you familiar with the phrase 'just the tip of the iceberg'?"

They nodded.

"It's kind of like that. Over the past few decades, scientists studying the age of the universe noticed strange behaviors in the way galaxies spin. The only thing we can think of that might account for these quirks is greater gravitational fields resulting from far more mass in the universe than seems possible. Dark matter, in other words, is matter we can't detect except by its effects on the matter we can see."

He pulled a pitcher from the center of the table and poured a cup of coffee. Emptying a packet of sugar into his palm, he continued. "Let's say this sugar is the universe we know, the matter we can see."

He poured the sugar into the coffee. The grains vanished into its blackness.

"And the coffee is dark matter. It's all around the matter, and there is far more of it. Some think as much as ninety-nine percent of the matter in the universe is dark matter.

"Now, your grandfather and a few others have been exploring theories that suggest that not only is most of the universe hidden to us, but that dark matter itself is the stuff of *other* universes next to ours, all around ours, even *within* ours, but not part of ours. Some even believe there may be a way to open a window into the dark matter universes. That's what he was here to speak about."

"Do you know what he might have done following his presentation?" Doc asked. "Did he stay around the university?"

"I really have no idea. The last I saw of him was at the reception afterward. He spent the whole time talking with Carlos Gongoro, one of the graduate students."

"Is Carlos studying dark matter?"

"No, he's actually a biophysics student. He works on something to do with frogs, I believe."

SEVENTEEN

Carlos Gongoro was from the Republic of Hidalgo, a South American country nestled in the vast region between Brazil, Colombia, and Peru. It was a land of rain forests and mountains, with the mighty Amazon River rushing west to east through its heart.

Carlos was a biophysics student at Harvard, researching the effects of pollution on frogs. In recent years, frog populations around the world have steeply fallen due to the steady increase of industrial pollutants in the air and water. Carlos was apparently interested in saving the frogs.

As far as could be determined, no one had seen Carlos since the reception following Grandpa Wilde's speech on dark matter.

The Wildes couldn't be sure where Grandpa Wilde or Carlos Gongoro had gone. But a good amount of circumstantial evidence pointed in a clear direction. There were strange frogs involved, Grandpa Wilde had last been seen with Carlos Gongoro, Carlos studied frogs, and the image of Grandpa in the frog cave clearly showed a jungle environment that could very well belong to Hidalgo, the country Carlos was from.

All roads seemed to lead to Hidalgo, so to Hidalgo they flew.

EIGHTEEN

During the lengthy flight to South America, Brian and Wren researched Hidalgo using the *Colibri*'s onboard computer, connected via satellite to the network in Lyonesse. They studied what they could find of its history (very little), read all its published folklore (not much), scanned for news reports (they found a couple), and studied its maps (which seriously lacked detail). Reading Hidalgan travel brochures, they found them to be written so generically that they might have been describing any number of Central or South American countries.

This country was obscure in every way. So obscure, it almost seemed deliberate.

Deep within Hidalgo's dense rain forest, a jumble of low buildings crowded the banks of the Rio Verde, a tributary of the mighty Amazon. Most of the structures looked tired and faded, as if abandoned years ago. The streets were paved with old stones and choked with weeds, and the wilderness grasped the town with long fingers of jungle growth.

This weathered town was Verde Grande, the capital city of Hidalgo due to the fact it was the *only* city in Hidalgo. And that's being generous with the word *city*.

Visitors usually came to Verde Grande by the river. The river was also the closest thing to an airfield here; a plane required pontoons if it wanted to land.

When the silent autogyro appeared above the town, word spread and the eyes of Verde Grande turned skyward.

As the residents looked up, Wren and Brian Wilde looked down. They saw townsfolk pour into the streets like agitated ants pouring from a damaged hill.

"Think they see us?" Wren asked.

"Maybe they're having a fire drill," Brian replied.

Declan hovered over the river, where a weathered wooden bridge connected the two sides of the town. A few people ran onto the bridge for a better look at their odd aerial visitor. Thanks to an external microphone on the autogyro, the Wildes heard an indistinct buzz of Spanish chatter.

"Speak up if you see something that seems out of place," Doc called back from the copilot seat.

The only three-story building in the town was a large villa, uncharacteristically expansive and elegant compared to the other structures. It faced an open plaza that served as the town square. Unless some millionaire had retired to Verde Grande and built his dream house, this was where they'd find the local authority.

The *Colibri* touched down in the square with all the noise of a moth alighting on a down pillow.

Brian and Wren undid their straps, eager to get outside and explore. Their father looked back at them from the copilot's seat. "Wait," he commanded. "It's unlikely, but the local population may be hostile."

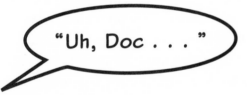

Declan mac Coul said, pointing out the window. "You may be right."

The kids moved to the cockpit. Bartlett joined them, and the whole crew watched through the windshield.

A squad of soldiers swarmed from the villa, forming a precise line between it and the *Colibri*. Some held AK-47 assault rifles. Some shouldered rocket launchers.

They each dropped to a knee and took aim.

NINETEEN

The soldiers menacing the _Colibri_ looked deadly serious, ready to open fire at any second. They wore olive-drab fatigues, baseball-style military caps casting shadows over their eyes. Civilian townsmen were gathering at the edges of the plaza, and they too carried AK-47 assault rifles.

"A town militia," Doc Wilde explained. "A country with such a small population wouldn't have a large military, so citizens provide the backup."

"That, or the whole town's camouflage for a supervillain lair," Declan said.

"What now, Dad?" Wren asked.

"I'll go outside. The rest of you, stay in here. You'll be a lot safer and can always fly off if you have to. They're probably just acting defensively."

The kids stepped back to let Doc leave the cockpit. In the cabin, he slipped off his vest and holster.

"You're going unarmed?" Brian asked.

"I need to seem as nonthreatening as possible," Doc replied.

They watched as he unsealed the hatch. They trusted their father's instincts implicitly, but he'd be stepping right in front of a wall of guns with no cover. They couldn't help feeling nervous.

He pulled the hatch door open. "Lock it behind me," he told them. "And don't open it until I say to or until you're somewhere safe."

Doc stepped out to the ground below, and Brian closed the door.

TWENTY

In the *Colibri's* cockpit, Wren and Brian crowded
Declan as they watched what was happening outside.
They saw a ripple of anxiety, perhaps even fear, cross the
faces of the gathered soldiers as Doc Wilde stood before
them, towering over even the tallest man among them,
the tropical sun shining from his golden skin and hair,
glittering in his strange eyes.

The villa doors opened, and a man bounded down
the steps, darting to the nearest soldier and wrenching the rifle from the soldier's hands. The new man
tossed the AK-47 to the ground with apparent derision
and made a broad, downward sweep with his hands.
"Bajar tus armas!" Lower your weapons!

The soldiers obeyed.

The man walked forward, arms open in greeting, a
warm smile on his tanned face. He had a pencil-thin
mustache and wore a short-sleeved white shirt, dark
green slacks, and leather sandals. On one wrist, a gold
watch shone in the tropical sun.

Those in the gyro watched as Doc Wilde met him halfway between the *Colibri* and the villa. The Hidalgan offered his hand, and Doc shook it. They talked a minute, then Doc nodded and strode back to the gyro, giving an "all-clear" signal with his hand.

Wren and Brian darted to the hatch and yanked it open.

Doc put a strong arm around each of the kids as he reentered the aircraft. "I think we're safe. That man is the *caudillo*, the political-military leader of all Hidalgo. He's also Carlos Gongoro's uncle."

TWENTY-ONE

"Brian Wilde! Wren Wilde!" Carlos's uncle called as Doc led his crew from the *Colibri*. "Welcome to Verde Grande!"

He shook Brian's hand, then Wren's. "You know who we are?" Wren asked.

"*Sí*, of course I know who you are; I have seen you on the news sometimes. Few others here will, however. I have the only satellite TV in Hidalgo. And these two gentlemen will naturally be the 'dashing' Phineas Bartlett and the 'shaggy' Declan mac Coul."

The dashing Phineas Bartlett looked at the shaggy Declan mac Coul and smiled hugely.

Don Rodrigo Gongoro was in charge of all of Hidalgo. Brian took note of the man's title: *caudillo*. It was an old Spanish term sometimes used in Latin America to designate a leader who controlled the country militarily as well as politically. They could just as easily be called *el presidente* or *generalissimo* and were sometimes fair leaders but all too often dominated their people with the iron hand of a dictator.

Their research on Hidalgo had turned up so little, they'd only known it was supposedly a republic. But that didn't mean much. Over the years, many so-called republics in this part of the world had actually been dictatorships.

This *caudillo* seemed friendly. But the quick obedience his men showed to his orders could indicate that he maintained discipline more strongly than might be necessary in such a small settlement.

TWENTY-TWO

They gathered in the villa's library with Don Rodrigo Gongoro, grouped around a small table upon which the *caudillo* had spread several maps. Doc had produced the photograph of Grandpa in the frog cave, and it now lay among the maps. He had decided to share that much; the Hidalgan leader might be able to point them in the right direction. No one had said so, but the kids knew that they shouldn't mention the emerald frog (which was stashed on the *Colibri* in a well-shielded secret compartment, more secure than any safe). That was of unknown significance, and they knew *someone* wanted it.

"Do you know where that cave is, sir?" Brian asked Don Rodrigo.

"I am afraid not," the *caudillo* said. "As I explained to your father, the first I heard of such a place was from my nephew when he brought your grandfather here."

"Grandpa was here?" the kids asked in unison.

Don Rodrigo chuckled at their stereo effect. "Yes. He and Carlos planned to go to this cave. Carlos showed me a sketch he'd done of it. He did a good job; it looked exactly like this photograph. I suppose he may have been there. . . . If so, I have no idea how he got there or when." The Hidalgan's face turned serious. "I tried to discourage them from going."

"Why?" Wren asked.

"The cave is somewhere in the northern jungles. We have no useful maps of that area; it is mostly unexplored . . . and very dangerous."

"Dangerous how?" Brian asked.

"Numerous expeditions have gone there over the centuries and never returned. My people have many old stories they tell of those jungles. They tell of monsters. I do not believe in monsters, but perhaps there *are* incredibly dangerous animals there."

He paused, staring at the photograph of the cave. Then he looked up at them, and his face was stern, but his eyes shone with held-back tears.

"Those jungles swallow people. I fear they have swallowed our loved ones."

TWENTY-THREE

The Amazon rain forest spread beneath the Wilde party, a shimmering carpet of many shades of green spiced with all the vivid colors of the rainbow. Streamers of cloud floated across its canopy like long, lazy ghosts.

They'd learned all they could from Don Rodrigo, and Verde Grande was behind them. Now they were bound toward the mysterious northern jungles of Hidalgo and, hopefully, toward finding Grandpa Wilde and Carlos Gongoro safe.

Declan brought the *Colibri* in low over the trees, slowing so they could make out details: flowers, vines, monkeys. A fine spatter of rain misted the windows, giving the view an otherworldly shimmer.

"I love it here," Wren said in a whisper.

"Me too," Doc said.

They had been to the great rain forests of South America several times before (in Peru and Brazil, but not Hidalgo), and it was an environment that could never grow boring. Here, there was more life per square mile than in any other location on the planet. Here, civilizations had risen to greatness and fallen to silence. Here, there were endless adventures, lost tribes, strange beasts, fabled cities of gold . . .

A flock of birds rose ahead of them, gracefully swooping. Brian squinted, trying to see what species they were, but the sun was in his eyes. By the time the autogyro was close enough for him to see the birds, he could see that they *weren't* birds at all. **They were frogs.**

But as you might suspect, they were not your average everyday little croakers, nor were they the stickily intense spy frogs. Like the spy frogs and man-frogs, however, they were unlike any creatures previously known to science.

For frogs, they were huge, about the size of house cats. They were actually quite beautiful, multicolored, with stripes and speckles of bright red, blue, violet, orange. Their legs were long and spindly, and the forelegs swept out in full, flapping, batlike wings. And their snouts had hardened, sharpened into flesh-tearing beaks like those of carnivorous birds.

There were at least a couple dozen of them, and they swarmed the *Colibri* like airborne piranha.

"Uh, Doc . . . " Declan said as three of the amphibians smacked onto the windshield before him, their talons and beaks scratching at the virtually unbreakable glass.

Doc Wilde unbuckled his seat belt and moved to the cockpit, crouching between Declan and Bartlett. "Amazing," he said.

"Holy smokes!" Brian shouted, looking out his porthole right into the face of one of the frogs.

Wren tried to peer past her brother. "We must be going the right way."

"Unless this is an astronomical coincidence," Phineas Bartlett said, "I would have to say you're correct."

The *Colibri* was so quiet they could hear the frenzied cries of the creatures, **CRRRAAAWWWKKK! CRRRAAAWWK!** It was somewhere between an amphibian croak and an eagle's piercing call.

Dull thuds resonated through the hull as more of the frogs grabbed on.

"Go faster," Doc told Declan. "Very fast."

The burly Irishman pulled back the stick and poured on the power. The autogyro shot higher into the sky, the great rotor whirling with tornado speed.

Several of the flying frogs were left in their wake, screeching angrily, unable to catch up.

Most of them, however, had already landed on the flying machine and were holding on hungrily.

"Bloody frogs," Declan growled.

TWENTY-FOUR

The Colibri, like all of Doc Wilde's self-made vehicles, was not only built of the strongest materials available, it had been coated with his polymer armor spray. The airborne frogs (probably) couldn't get in. On the other hand, neither the craft's incredible speed as they rocketed over the rain forest nor the deft maneuvers of pilot Declan mac Coul had managed to dislodge even one of the creatures clinging to the hull.

So, the humans and the frogs were at a stalemate. Except for one thing: Doc and his crew would have to land eventually, and once they left the vehicle, they would likely be savaged by the beaked killers.

"Should we parachute?" Phineas Bartlett asked.

"I think they'd just fly down and eat us in midair," Brian answered.

Doc Wilde nodded. "Yes, I'm certain they would. Right now, it seems our only advantage is that we're inside the *Colibri.*"

"I could crash," Declan said. "Maybe into a lake . . . "

Wren wrinkled her nose in a scowl. "They're *frogs*, Declan. They'll probably be just as dangerous in the water. Besides, I hate when we crash."

"Could we fly higher and freeze them off?" Brian asked.

His dad smiled. "An excellent idea, Brian!"

He turned to Declan. "Take her up to twelve thousand feet."

Declan spiraled the *Colibri* skyward,

UP, UP, UP . . .

"Nine thousand . . . ten . . . eleven . . . "

Far below, the carpet of green spread in all directions, cut in places with bright blue ribbons of water. In the distance, their snowy peaks looming far higher than the autogyro now flew, the Andes mountains stood majestic and beautiful.

Here, at twelve thousand feet, the temperature was just over sixteen degrees Fahrenheit, sixteen degrees below freezing.

Frogs are cold-blooded, meaning that their bodies

take on the temperature of the environment around them rather than creating heat and maintaining a constant temperature, as mammals do. As a result, frogs don't do well when it gets cold and do *very* badly when subjected to freezing temperatures. At twelve thousand feet, the flying flesh eaters fared no better than any run-of-the-mill Mississippi bullfrog would have.

Inside the *Colibri*, Doc and his crew listened as the hungry **CRRRRAAAWWWKs** thinned, then fell silent. Now they heard an eerie rattling noise, and when they looked at the frogs on the windshield, they saw what was causing the sound:

The frogs' beaks were chattering.

In time, that noise too passed, leaving just the roar of the passing wind.

The frogs on the windshield no longer so much as twitched, and their eyes and skin started growing a grayish sheen of frost.

"Stay up here for now," Doc told Declan. "They could still be alive, in suspended animation. I want them to freeze solid, just to make sure."

"Once they're dead for sure, can I have one?" Wren asked.

"Me too," Brian said. He was thinking how cool one

of these things would look stuffed and hanging over his bed at home.

Doc Wilde laughed. "Sure. I'll keep a couple myself. It'll be a fascinating study."

"You can have 'em," Declan said. "I prefer my amphibians on the ground, where they belong."

A long sputtering noise vibrated through the *Colibri*'s frame.

"Uh-oh," Declan said.

The engine burped to a stop.

"Uh-oh, indeed," Bartlett said. "It appears you'll soon be in the trees, where *you* belong."

Doc jumped back to his seat. "Make sure you're buckled in—

we're going down!"

TWENTY-FIVE

When Dr. Spartacus Wilde builds something,
he builds it well. His devices, machines, and inventions are as fine as Swiss clockwork, sturdy as an iron safe. All the same, nothing in this universe is perfect, and where chaos can poke its multifarious hydra heads, it will.

The *Colibri* was nigh impenetrable, bulletproof, able to survive the blast of a large artillery shell, waterproof to twenty fathoms (though not particularly maneuverable underwater), even resistant to electricity, making it pretty much lightning proof.

There's something called an electromagnetic pulse that occurs when a nuclear weapon explodes, and it fries any and all electronics within its zone. Doc didn't use electronics; he used various highly developed forms of nanotechnology (complex devices of submolecular size, some as small as a human hair's growth in the time it takes to blink). The carbon-based nanotech he used in much of the *Colibri* was resistant to EMP and, combined with the radiation shielding on the gyro, made it capable of resisting a small nuclear blast. (As long as it wasn't very close.)

One thing he hadn't counted on, however, was **gremlipoles**.

The ferocious flying frogs had been purposefully infested with these things before being sent after the autogyro. The gremlipoles were the tadpole form of tiny creatures called **gremlitoads**.

If machines have an archenemy, it's gremlitoads. They are the size of dimes, and if they get into an engine, be it a tractor, car, or plane, they ooze a powerful acid that dissolves metal and plastics, effectively digesting it *before* eating it. No normal engine can stand against an infestation of gremlitoads.

Gremlitoads wouldn't have been able to penetrate the autogyro's hull (built from carbon nanotube-infused graphite, a material one-sixth the weight of steel but over one hundred times as strong), but their spawn are more insidious.

The gremlipoles are microscopic in size, smaller than germs, and share their adult forms' delight in the taste of machinery. Carried onto the *Colibri* by the flying frogs and sensing the metal in the craft, the gremlipoles poured eagerly from their carriers.

They couldn't break through the armor coating sprayed over the hull, but they wriggled over the outside of the craft, instinctively seeking a way in. They found it in a single, somewhat loose bolt on the engine casing. As Doc and the others tried to decide how to deal with the flyers, the little wrigglers slipped past the bolt and made their way deep within, safe inside as the temperature outside started to fall.

Their acid was ineffective against the primary devices of the autogyro, which were made with nanotechnology. The large, moving parts of the engine, however, were a different story.

The *Colibri* was the latest in a line of Wilde-built autogyros dating back to Grandpa's adventures in the first half of the twentieth century. As newer versions were built, still-functional components had often been cannibalized from earlier models because the Wildes avoided waste as much as possible. This craft had inherited some mechanical elements from its immediate ancestor, which had been built before the development of the nanotech-based material Doc now used instead of metal. These parts were forged from superalloy steel.

The gremlipoles got into these and oozed their acid, eating through the metal with gusto. As the *Colibri* cruised at twelve thousand feet, the creatures' buffet destroyed the engine's workings, and it stopped.

The adventurers inside knew none of this (though Doc would piece it together later); all they knew was that the autogyro had somehow lost its engine.

Oh, and that it was falling.

TWENTY-SIX

The powerless *Colibri* fell toward the dense rain forest below.

"I'm hungry," Wren said.

"We'll eat something after we crash," Doc told her.

At the controls, Declan mac Coul absently whistled a sweet Irish tune.

"There aren't any settlements near here, are there?" Brian asked.

"No," Doc said. "It looks like we'll get a great tour of the rain forest."

In the seat next to Declan, Phineas Bartlett quietly read a book, *City of the Beasts*, by Isabel Allende.

Doc peered thoughtfully out the porthole. *After dissecting those frogs, did I turn off the Bunsen burner . . . ?*

Had they been in an airplane or helicopter, the group would have been very concerned, possibly terrified. But one of the reasons Doc Wilde used an autogyro instead now saved their lives.

Unlike an airplane, it is impossible for a gyro to stall

or go into a spin. If it loses forward momentum for some reason, it will just drop. Like a pinwheel, its rotor gains spin as it rushes through air and acts as a parachute, wafting the craft gently to ground. The fall is so soft, the pilot can steer it to the safest available landing.

They were close now, the trees of the rain forest taking on individual shape rather than blurring into a field of green. Declan swung the gyro around, looking for a clearing to set it down in, but he wasn't seeing anything. The thick jungle stretched unbroken for miles.

They could settle in the canopy, but it wouldn't be a comfortable landing, and they'd have to rappel down the 150-foot trees.

If they'd been over one of the countries bordering the Republic of Hidalgo, they might've found a spot to land in a slash-and-burn clear-cut left behind by some big timber company. But because the government of Hidalgo stubbornly protected its rain forests, there were no clear-cuts here.

That was fine by Declan, though. He'd rather crash into a rock than benefit from such scarring of the earth.

"Look west," Doc told him. "There's a large lake. We can land there."

Declan drifted westward, and the lake grew in their

sight, a vast sheet of blue dappled with stars of sunlight. He took the gyro down, banking in close to the shore.

The *Colibri* landed like a feather. It sloshed gently from side to side on the water, flying frogs still frozen to its hull like warts. It was a simple matter to row it to the lake's edge to unload their equipment and provisions.

TWENTY-SEVEN

The fight was swift and deadly but so small it could only be seen through an atomic nanoscope, a rare device with submolecular magnification even greater than that of an electron microscope.

Doc Wilde had one, pocket size, which he carried in his utility vest. His kids took turns peering through it, watching the microcosmic battle with glee.

It took Doc fifteen minutes to determine the cause of the *Colibri*'s engine malfunction, and he labeled the minute saboteurs "gremlipoles" because of their resemblance to tadpoles. He would realize the utter appropriateness of the name only upon encountering their adult forms, which he'd call "gremlitoads" (oddly enough, that wouldn't happen until another adventure a long, long way from here).

As a way of preventing the possible spread of the gremlipoles to other gear (uncertain if their corrosive effect was confined to metal), Doc had taken a small vial from one of the many pockets on his vest. Inside was a glittering powder, finer than dust. He tipped a dash of the powder into the open engine casing, then returned the vial to his pocket.

This powder was a wondrous example of Doc's nanotechnology. The dash of powder he poured was actually trillions of "nanites," nanotech robots designed with one purpose: the elimination of harmful microorganisms from a person or place.

Each of these nanites possessed an amazingly sophisticated computer mind that could identify all known microorganisms that were beneficial to human life. Such microbes would be ignored, safe to continue their duties in the great biological scheme of things.

Harmful (or unknown) agents, however, were in trouble. If the nanites encountered malign bacteria or parasitic infestation, they attacked the germs, worms, or whatever else they might be with the ferocity of a jaguar falling upon a wild pig. The nanites would fasten themselves to the harmful infection or infestation, killing it and self-destructing at the same time.

This trait—and a life span deliberately limited to five minutes outside a living host, fifteen inside—kept the robots from running amok through the world, eliminating not only bad germs and such but any manner of things we might not want them to eliminate.

Doc carried the powder as a first aid measure because a pinch of it sprinkled in a wound would not only eliminate all chance of infection but would clear up any bacterial illness a person might be suffering.

Also, in foreign environments the Wildes routinely sprinkled the powder into their rations for protection against diseases and exotic parasites that might take up residence in their systems.

The dust wasn't perfect. Doc hadn't yet made it work against viruses and cancers, and the nanites were made of silver, platinum, and gold, making their production horrifyingly expensive. But it was possible that these tiny robots would one day be a universal cure for all disease, hopefully at a cost low enough to make their widespread use practical.

For the moment, however, they were making hash of the gremlipoles infesting the autogyro. It was this battle Brian and Wren Wilde were watching through the pocket nanoscope.

While the gremlipoles met their tiny dooms, Doc, Declan, and Bartlett unloaded everyone's field gear from the autogyro and discussed their possible courses of action.

The damage to the *Colibri*'s engine was so extensive it needed to be replaced; they'd have to go after Grandpa

Wilde on foot. The original plan had been to fly to the feet of the Andes mountains, on the assumption that was a likely area for a cave. They would have then used the *Colibri* and its scanners to swiftly scout the area.

Wandering blindly through endless miles of jungle, hoping to run into the kids' grandfather in a coincidence worthy of a pulp magazine story, didn't seem like a good strategy. But as far as they knew, Verde Grande, nearly a hundred miles to the southeast, was the nearest human settlement. Their GPS units would keep them on track, but it was still a long walk.

Doc Wilde decided keeping to the mission was the most important thing; the more time passed, the more likely something bad might happen to his father. So they'd make for the mountains, then search as well as they could.

Hopefully, they'd make it without first being eaten by frogs.

TWENTY-EIGHT

"Let's go, kids," Doc Wilde said, and Wren and Brian raced to put on their field gear, ready to get moving.

Aside from the gadgets in the Wildes' vests and equipment and provisions in each person's pack, the team's bulkier items (including three dead flying frogs vacuum-packed for later study) were loaded into a bigger backpack. The adults would alternate carrying it; Declan hefted it now.

Then, for a full minute or more, the crew stood without words, gazing into the immeasurable depths of the rain forest around them.

"'The walking of which I speak,'" Phineas Bartlett quoted softly, "'has nothing in it akin to taking exercise, as it is called, as the sick take medicine at stated hours, but is itself the enterprise and adventure of the day.'"

"Henry David Thoreau," Wren said.

"In . . . ?" her father asked.

"*Walden* or his essay 'Walking,'" Brian broke in. "Probably 'Walking.'"

"'Walking' it is," Bartlett affirmed.

"And walking we are," Doc Wilde said.

The jungle around them was an odd mixture of yawning cathedral-like space and looming forest. Enormous trees rose like Gothic columns, crowding the edges of vision, their brawny roots woven across the ground everywhere like a field of dozing serpents.

It was murky. Most of the sunlight was absorbed by the dense canopy, which stretched unbroken far above like a second forest overlaying this one.

A constant background of chirruping insects, peeping frogs (normal, everyday, Amazonian frogs as far as they could tell), chattering monkeys, and a thousand different birdcalls filled what, nonetheless, seemed like a grand silence. There was no sign of civilization here. The world about them was electric with primal life, the forest of dreams and memories from ancestral minds.

A soft, warm rain fell. They donned crushable felt fedoras but no rain gear. Their clothes were cotton, which would have gotten drenched and stayed wet in the extreme humidity, but thanks to a special treatment shed water like a duck's feathers and stayed dry.

They trudged on. The bumpiness of the ground underfoot made hiking slower and more strenuous. It was going to be a long while before they saw a human settlement again.

They stopped to camp after a couple of hours, as the murk around them darkened even more. Each took to a task: Wren and Brian erected the large tent and inflated sleeping mats. Declan prepared the food, while Bartlett lit camp lights. Doc Wilde sliced open thick liana vines and drained them of a surprisingly large amount of fresh water, capturing it in a collapsible water bag. Clean drinking water wouldn't be a problem.

Then the kids joined Doc beneath a tree for their daily exercises. These were a key part of their developmental regimen, and, just like their father and grandfather, they had done some variation of this routine every day of their lives. This program was developed by Grandpa Wilde's father and a brain trust of genius experts before Grandpa had even been born. Grandpa, and later Doc, expanded and refined the exercises in the years since.

First, the Wildes assumed what the Japanese call *seiza*, sitting on their heels with knees forward, and started a basic breath-counting meditation. To do this, you breathe slowly and deeply, relaxing all your muscles, counting each breath till you reach nine, then beginning the count again at one. If you lose focus and count past nine, restart at one and keep going. Doing this daily builds mental focus, and it's a starting point for even deeper meditative practices.

When their minds and bodies settled to a peaceful calm, the Wildes began their mental and sensory exercises. First, they closed their eyes and listened. They listened to every sound around and within them, every birdcall or monkey screech, every beetle scuttle, every thump of their own hearts, every whisper of breeze through leaves, every rattle of tree branches above.

After a while, they shifted focus to the other senses in turn, noticing as much information as they could with each. This sharpened the senses and strengthened the mind.

Then came their physical training. In the Lyceum at home, they had a full gymnasium of exercise machines and weights, as well as acrobatic and gymnastic equipment, but in the field they used a routine of stretches, isometrics, martial arts katas, rolls, and calisthenics to keep their bodies strong, tuned, and ready for action.

They did this for a while, tightening tendons, straining muscles, gracefully practicing moves both acrobatic and combative.

Some of the exercises their father did were still too difficult for the kids. They paused their own routines in amazement to watch him glide into different positions, looking forward to the day *they* could do *that*.

Upside down, Doc Wilde balanced on the fingertips of one hand, slowly scissoring his legs back and forth into full splits in the air. Yet his face showed no sign of exertion, his limbs did not quiver, his breath remained steady. Only a light sheen of sweat on his golden skin served as a clue that he was involved in what was probably the most strenuous exercise routine ever practiced by anyone on earth.

When the young Wildes were deeply focused, they often lost track of the world around them. But they knew that even in the deepest parts of his workout, their dad remained superhumanly aware of everything around him.

Indeed, when the session was complete, Doc gathered the team. "Stay alert," he said quietly. "There's something observing us, but I haven't figured out where it is yet."

TWENTY-NINE

In the deep night, everyone slept except for Declan mac Coul, who hunched beneath a canopy outside the tent listening to the jungle sounds and the soothing fall of soft rain.

All was peaceful, but Doc's warning that something or someone had been tracking them was fresh in Declan's mind, so he knew to keep his guard up. If something happened, a shout (or a slap to the alarm button on his belt) would instantly rouse the others to action.

As he crouched there, so apelike he seemed to belong in the jungle, Declan gradually grew aware of a slight scraping sound. He turned to see where it was coming from.

The backpack.

Something had gotten inside and had moved enough for him to hear. As he watched, the top flap on the pack undulated as things were pushed around beneath it.

Should he awaken Doc? It was probably some jungle

rodent or a snake. Might even be a gadget of Doc's, accidentally activated . . .

He'd check it first, then wake his friends if necessary.

He moved to the pack and squatted before it. Whatever was inside rustled louder, like it was digging for something.

Declan lifted the flap and gasped.

THIRTY

It was the emerald frog with ruby eyes.

It *had* been securely wrapped and tucked into a zippered pouch on the inner skin of the pack, but now it was atop the mound of gear. And it was giving off its own light, glowing brighter by the moment, bright enough to read by.

It was lovely. But this couldn't be good, not good at all.

But . . .

He hadn't realized before just how lovely it was . . .

Its presence was purest comfort, bringing peace to Declan's soul. Nothing else seemed to exist. *Lovely*. He *had* to clasp its loveliness to him.

He reached his big hand in and picked up the frog.

The green light pulsated brighter.

The frog was cold. Holding it was like holding an icicle. But to Declan, it was heavenly.

It squirmed in his grasp.

Its bloodred eyes blinked, and a black tongue of

shadow flicked from its maw, between rows of horrid teeth.

The emerald frog jumped from his hand to his head, its claws snagging in his thick red hair, settling in.

Declan mac Coul was gone, drifting in a place of happy, a place of lovely, a place of strangely pleasant freezing cold.

He stood, the frog blazing on his head like a heatless green flame.

He suddenly had a really great idea!

He drew his pistol. Smiling a smile that was in no way like his own, he entered the tent where the others slept.

He knew Doc Wilde was the most dangerous, so Declan shot him first.

THIRTY-ONE

Declan mac Coul's shot hit Doc Wilde in the chest.

The gun made nary a sound as it fired its high-speed dart. This dart contained a paralyzing agent that would put a man out of action for at least two hours but did no actual harm to its victim. Doc cherished life and despised unnecessary violence, so his team favored non-deadly weapons.

Declan shot Phineas Bartlett next, the dart hitting the majordomo in the neck.

The Irishman turned toward Wren and Brian and fired. A dart snagged in Wren's upper arm. She made a tiny cry before paralysis hit.

One to go.

He fired at Brian. But the boy had awakened at his sister's tiny cry next to him and, in the light from the glowing frog, saw Declan mac Coul aiming at him and rolled quickly to the side. The dart **THUNKED** into his sleeping mat, which started to deflate with a wheeze.

The gemstone frog atop Declan's head flared a brighter green as Declan swung the gun to get the boy in his sights again.

Brian jumped at the wall, drawing his knife and slicing a huge slit in the tent. He dove into the night, rolling to his feet as he heard another dart hit the tent wall behind him.

There was a bright flash of green and Declan grunted, as if annoyed.

Brian raced across the rough ground, hearing the stocky pilot thrash his way out of the tent. He ducked behind a huge tree, its trunk thick with vines.

It was so dark he could almost feel the texture of the darkness in the air. Rain poured steadily down. Looking back, Brian could see the campsite in the small circle of light thrown by the camp lantern. He could also see the greenish glow of whatever that thing was on Declan's head, moving around behind the tent as the burly man searched for him.

Brian analyzed the situation.

Something was somehow controlling Declan via the emerald frog. The Irishman had shot everyone but Brian. He was using his dart pistol, which meant the others were only paralyzed.

Everyone slept in their clothes in case of trouble, so

Brian was fully dressed except for his utility vest. Which, of course, meant he had none of his gear.

He did have his knife. It was always at his belt, so it'd been at hand when he needed to escape the tent. His father taught that a knife was a tool, foremost, and only a weapon in the most extreme circumstances. Brian had never used it as anything but a tool. And he wouldn't use it as a weapon on Declan mac Coul, his friend, who wasn't responsible for what he was doing.

The young Wilde was at a loss. The pilot was a short man but a solid slab of brawn, outweighing Brian by about two hundred pounds. And he had a gun.

How could Brian prevail against him?

THIRTY-TWO

The world was in motion under Wren, a rhythmic jouncing, and the space behind her closed eyes was a swirl of weird darkness. She could feel her limbs hanging like lead weights, muscles like thick putty, but something strong pinned her body and she knew she wouldn't be able to escape it easily. She felt a spike of fear, but it passed as she noticed a familiar and overwhelmingly comforting scent, a smell that meant safety: the close smell of her dad.

She opened her eyes.

The world returned to her, and as it did, so did the memory of where she was and what she was doing there.

The jungle moved around her, or, rather, she moved through the jungle.

It was just after dawn. No rain was falling, and a hint of sunlight filtered through the canopy. She felt a sudden yearning for a look at the sky.

She was safe in her father's arms. He held her against

his broad chest as he paced steadily through the green gloom of the rain forest.

He noticed her awakening. "Good morning," he said.

He lowered her gently to the ground, one of his hands holding her steady as she got her feet under her. She felt like she was standing on the deck of a ship in very choppy waters.

Now she saw that he also had Phineas Bartlett in a loose carry across his shoulders. A small laugh popped out of her at the sight of the ever-dapper Englishman's jaw hanging open, a slight line of saliva swinging from his lip. It would probably be best never to mention this to him.

She stopped laughing as she realized it was just the three of them.

"Where are Brian and Declan?" she asked.

"We're tracking them," Doc told her. He crouched and gingerly placed Bartlett on the ground. Bartlett groaned and his eyelids fluttered. "The dart antidote's kicking in. When he comes to, I'll tell you both what's going on."

A few minutes of murmurs, moans, and twitches later, Phineas Bartlett pushed himself up with wobbly arms. He glanced around. "What happened? Where are Brian and the Neanderthal?"

Doc explained.

"You think it was one of those frog guys?" Wren asked when he was done.

Doc Wilde frowned. "Perhaps. If so, I understand why it would take the emerald frog, because the frog is clearly important to them. I'm not sure how Brian and Declan factor in."

Ten minutes later, the trio were on the move again. Wren and Bartlett were still wobbly and could have used a longer break to recover, but their concern for those missing was too deep not to move as soon as they could.

The root-smothered ground and daytime twilight made tracking difficult, yet Doc Wilde's sharp eyes found tiny scrapes and impressions here and there, which kept them moving in the right direction. Fortunately, that direction was the way they'd been traveling already: north, away from civilization, deeper into the tropical wilderness, toward the towering Andes mountains (though they couldn't see them from beneath the thick cover of the rain forest).

By Wren's reckoning (and she was an expert orienteer), they were probably not far from the region they'd been flying over when they were attacked by the flying frogs.

By the time the three stopped for lunch, it became evident that something was astonishingly strange about this place. Their communicators were working fine, except for the fact that they couldn't pick up each other's signal, even if they were side by side. Similarly, their GPS navigation units no longer received data from the satellites. Even their basic old-fashioned magnetic-north compasses wouldn't point.

With the sun itself blocked by the forest canopy (preventing the simple east-west bearing they could have gotten from it), they could no longer determine exactly where they were.

They were lost in the jungle known in Hidalgan folklore as a land of nightmares.

A realm of MONSTERS.

THIRTY-THREE

Deeper in the uncharted jungles of Hidalgo, two figures made their way steadily north, a glowing emerald frog lighting their way through the murky shadows, its green light getting brighter with each mile they covered.

Brian kept back, out of sight, glad his father had trained him so well in the stealth of the ancient *shinobi*, the ninja. Knowing Declan would be long gone by the time any of the others awoke from the paralysis darts, Brian had decided to follow the big Irishman himself.

His hope had been to see where Declan was going, then return to camp. But after following for about an hour and a half, he was completely lost and knew he'd never manage to find his way back.

Brian and Wren had trained with aboriginal master trackers in places where hunting was still *the* essential life skill: the frozen forests of northern Norway with the Sami, the sweeping grasses of the Kenyan Serengeti with the Masai, even the misty rain forests of Washington with the Swinomish. Brian had considered following his own sign back to camp, but he hadn't had enough dirt time, time spent tracking in the wild, to be anywhere near expert. He'd likely get lost, meaning his dad would have two tough trails to track instead of one.

His father, however, was among the best trackers in the world; his only superiors *were* their tribal teachers, who tracked every day of their lives. Dad would eventually catch up. So Brian kept on Declan's trail.

He also used his father's amazing technology to make it easier for Doc to find his way. Recessed in the thin space between the leather and the sole of his right boot, so it wouldn't trigger accidentally, was a minute switch. Using the point of his knife, he flicked it and a small hole opened at the top of his heel. As he walked, every hundred steps what looked like a grain of sand popped out, leaving an intermittent trail among the madness of roots, stones, and tree litter covering the rain forest's floor.

The Wildes called these grains "bread crumbs." Leaving a subtle path, they were a backup measure for times the Wildes were separated and unable to use their communicators or GPS units to find each other again. Another type of nanite, the tiny, tiny devices glowed with a color so high in the ultraviolet spectrum it was invisible to the naked eye. The Wildes had special goggles that allowed them to see it. The bread crumbs would help Doc and the others catch up that much faster.

At the moment, though, Brian was getting even more worried about Declan.

The big man seemed almost to be sleep-walking, obviously driven by the emerald frog atop his head. He moved at a fair pace, but his steps fell heavily, his arms hung straight down, and he never looked anywhere but straight ahead.

At times, Brian crept a bit closer for a better view of Declan, and what he saw was alarming.

Declan's skin was turning green. At first, Brian hadn't been sure, thinking it was just the light from the frog, but after a time, it was clear that the greenish hue was darkening, even developing brownish spots. And Declan's fingers were lengthening, thinning, as his nails reshaped into claws. Worst of all, Declan's eyes were horrifically bloodshot with thickening webs of red and starting to grow, bulging from their sockets, already the size of tennis balls.

He was turning into a man-frog!

On they went, into the mysterious Amazonian reaches.

After a while, Declan's stodgy step grew clumsier.

Brian thought perhaps he was getting tired. That was good; maybe he'd have to stop to rest or collapse from exhaustion. Brian was certainly getting worn out.

Declan stopped and fell on his butt. Yes! Now Dad would have more time to catch up.

The mutating Irishman wrested off his shoes. His feet seemed to flap out, the toes long, webbed, and clawed. He stood. Then he hopped.

Brian frowned. Oh, that was just great.

THIRTY-FOUR

The God of Frogs knew the boy was following. Of course It did. This was Its Kingdom on Earth, after all, and It knew everything that happened here. It saw and It heard because the jungles of Its kingdom were inhabited by thousands of the not-too-bright but highly useful spy frogs.

It ignored the small male, clearly no threat. When the remaining three mammals entered the kingdom, however, It was annoyed. Overall, they were no danger, but there was something about the big male that seemed . . . troubling.

It had sent warriors to rescue the emerald key from the mammals. The warriors failed their mission, but the stupid warm-bloods brought the key to the jungle anyway; when the key was close enough to the kingdom, It spoke unto the key, awakening the mystic artifact, impelling the key to seize a host.

After so long, the key would soon be here. It would

use the key to open the thick skin of the Dark, allowing
It to eat the light from this world.

There was no way the mammals could hinder It.

Yet still, that big male vexed It.

So It decided to send Its beasts to deal with him.

THIRTY-FIVE

The jungle that Doc Wilde, Wren, and Bartlett moved through was murkier than before, a dark gloam heavy with mist. The rain had started again. The trail they followed was a line of infrequent, tiny deviations in the environment: a slight heel scuff on a rough-skinned root, a pebble disturbed, a footprint in the spongy mulch so shallow Wren couldn't make it out even when her dad pointed to it.

Wren and her dad wore strange goggles, made of a rubbery polymer so soft and breathable that they barely felt them against their skin. This eyewear had various useful settings, one of which let them see the soft purple glow emitted by the nanite bread crumbs spat from Brian's heel. Led by the light of these grains, the adventurers made swifter progress, secure in the knowledge that they were still following the correct trail.

As they discovered the bread crumbs, Wren collected them in a pouch on her belt. As she helped her dad look for sign, her heightened senses told her the rain forest around them was changing in ways she couldn't define, becoming *stranger*. More *sinister*.

She felt the stares of many eyes. It didn't take her long to spot the numerous fat spy frogs scattered in the brush or stuck on trees.

It had been a while since she'd seen or heard any of the previously ever-present monkeys or seen a rodent skitter from their path, or a sloth oozing through the branches, or the track of a wild pig. She heard no birdsong.

It seemed they were the only warm-blooded creatures in the jungle.

"This place is creepy," Wren said.

"'In the middle of the journey of our life I came to myself within a dark wood where the straight way was lost,'" Bartlett quoted. "Dante, *Divine Comedy*."

"'But on you will go though the weather be foul,'" Wren quoted. "'On you will go though your enemies prowl. On you will go though the Hakken-Kraks howl . . . '"

Bartlett looked at her. "My goodness, you've stumped me. What *is* that?"

Doc Wilde grinned.

"Dr. Seuss," Wren replied, grinning like her dad. *"Oh, the Places You'll Go!"*

"Marvelous," said Phineas Bartlett with a smile.

And on they went.

Though their enemies prowled.

As they got deeper into the uncharted realm, terrain that had been relatively level now started to rise and fall. The ground swelled higher with each passing mile as they reached the foothills of the Andes. Travel that was rough became rougher, slowing their progress. If those they followed didn't stop soon, or at least stop for a long break, Doc's group might not catch up before night fell.

Doc spurred Wren and Bartlett on as quickly as they could go without exhausting themselves. Wren knew that alone, he could have raced ahead, but that would further divide the crew, making it that much more difficult to unite and defend.

In the late afternoon, they were resting before fording a river (it would be the third they'd had to cross so far) when Wren smelled a strange odor, very weak, drifting through the humid air. The smell was like stagnant water, but she knew immediately it came off something alive.

She glanced at her dad; he was already looking her way because he smelled it too. Bartlett, lacking the intensely trained senses of the Wilde family, did not.

"Phineas," Doc whispered, "on your guard."

The majordomo nodded and scanned the surrounding brush, whipping the slender blade from his sword cane.

Doc and Wren drew their dart pistols.

A horrifying roar shattered the forest calm, and **something monstrous exploded from the bushes.**

THIRTY-SIX

The beast was, of course, a frog, but a frog the size of a St. Bernard, with bear-paw-size claws, a spiky sail fin down its back like a spinosaurus, and enormous fangs jutting straight down from its upper jaw.

A saber-toothed frog.

The monster went right at Wren, but she did a perfect dive roll underneath its belly. It hit the ground with a snarl, just past where she'd been standing.

Doc fired three darts into the creature's back as it whirled around to face them.

The beast roared, jiggling its massive body in a fruitless attempt to shake off the annoying darts. Doc and Wren peppered its slick hide with more, enraging it further.

Phineas Bartlett lunged, stabbing just behind its foreleg with his sword.

It *really* didn't like that.

It spun to face him, sweeping that foreleg back against the sword, knocking it from Bartlett's hand, then leaped upon him, its two hundred or more pounds slamming him to the ground.

The darts didn't seem to be working.

Fearlessly, Doc threw himself at the monster, trying to get a hold on it, which was difficult because of its slimy skin and the jagged sail down its spine. He managed to shove the monster off Bartlett with his uncanny strength, leaping swiftly out of range as the frog slashed at him with its enormous fangs.

Bartlett took the opportunity to scramble away.

The beast crouched facing them. Its huge mouth gaped in another bone-rattling roar. Then it leaped at Doc Wilde.

Doc dodged, throwing a series of fast, hard punches into the soft tissues along its side and jarring its innards, the force of the blows driving it sideways and off-kilter.

It crashed to the earth so hard its body compressed like a squeezed water balloon, all the air forced from its lungs in a bellow of spit and bile.

Amazingly, the saber-toothed nightmare tried to rise to its feet. But it was wobbly and dazed.

Wren yanked a small metallic cylinder from one of her vest pockets and jumped to the beast's side. Its head lurched toward her quicker than she'd thought possible in its state; only a reflexive twist of her body saved her from its fangs.

Swift as a mongoose, she slammed the cylinder—which the Wildes called a "Thor stick"—into the space between the monster's eyes. Tiny prongs snapped out of the gadget, catching in the clammy skin. Wren let go and rolled out of the predator's reach.

Electricity coursed from the Thor stick, zapping through every cell of the frog's body. It hit the ground like a bag of mud, the spiked sail up its back aquiver, its nervous system overloaded. Its strong legs kicked once in unison, then went limp, its eyes rolling in different directions. It was still alive, breathing shallowly, but it wouldn't be moving anytime soon.

"'Beware the Jabberwock, my son!'" Bartlett said. "'The jaws that bite, the claws that catch!'"

"'Jabberwocky,' Lewis Carroll!" Wren shouted, nearly hopping because she was so charged with adrenaline.

Doc laughed. "Good job, kiddo."

As Bartlett cleaned his sword and returned it to its cane sheath, Doc bent over the felled beast for a closer look.

Wren started to join him, then shouted "Dad!"

Three more saber-toothed frogs burst from the rushing river and charged.

THIRTY-SEVEN

Declan paused in his leaping, and Brian slumped against a tree, happy for the rest. The big man wasn't in his line of sight, but the boy wasn't worried about losing track of him: the glowing frog atop Declan's head had reached spotlight intensity.

They were high in the foothills, where blisters of mossy stone broke through the jungle floor. The Declan man-frog's new hopping feet were very useful as he ascended hills in short bounds rather than having to hike the rugged slopes step by step. His awkward sluggishness was gone, replaced with a burning vitality.

Oddly, the creature the Irishman was becoming, though similar to the man-frogs the Wildes had encountered, seemed a more brutish variety, his skin darker and rough, his claws larger, and his bulging eyes now crimson instead of yellow.

As he rested, Brian gradually became aware of a change in the jungle sounds. Like his sister, he'd quickly sensed the unearthly qualities of this area, the lack of mammalian life, the loss of birdsong to an increased chorus of amphibian peeps and croaks.

Now that chorus seemed to swell, and he caught bits of motion in the periphery of his sight. He leaned forward, watching more intently. There was movement all around him. **FROGS.**

They seethed from the brush, from the trees, down hanging vines, advancing in hops like an army of popcorn popping through the jungle.

Brian stood, alarmed. The frogs all seemed to be normal jungle species of various sizes and colors, but their behavior was anything but normal. And their ranks were thickening around him.

Feeling the need for a weapon, he drew his knife. It wasn't going to be very useful against a hopping swarm of tiny amphibians, but he used it to cut a three-foot length from a woody vine (taking a quick drink as fresh water poured out). It was more flexible than a proper *hanbo,* or half staff, but better than nothing.

Suddenly, the small frogs started hopping into his hair, onto his shoulders, a tiny rain of frogs from the tree above. He jumped away from the trunk, dropping the staff and frantically batting at the things with his hands.

He managed to knock them off, but even as he did, scores more reached him, boiling around his feet like a biblical plague.

But they weren't attacking him. He was only an obstacle in their way. He stood still, watching the rainbow-colored swarm hop by, oblivious to him except as something to get past. Among their number were a few of the bloated spy frogs, but they didn't even look in his direction.

The frogs were converging on the bright green glow. On Declan.

Trying to avoid stepping on the little critters, Brian crept toward the glow. Not crushing them became tougher as he got closer because they were so thick on the ground they were hopping over each other in a literal game of leapfrog.

He crouched among them, peeking through the brush at the man-frog who had once been his friend. The emerald frog was so bright, Brian had to squint and shade his eyes with his hand.

Declan stood sweeping his claws over the gathering frogs as if blessing them; the hair went up on the back of Brian's neck as he guessed that was exactly what was happening.

The frogs were here to worship.

Declan had become their god.

Brian didn't know what to do. Standing in the midst of an army of clammy amphibians hopping in a religious frenzy was unsettling. But if he fled the scene, he wouldn't be able to see what was happening.

He was just about to decide to stay, knowing it was what his dad would do, when the decision was taken away from him.

Something shoved him from behind and he toppled forward, instinctively rolling, smooshing dozens of frogs, coming to his feet out in the open, facing his attacker.

ATTACKERS.

A gang of man-frogs hunched before him, big yellow eyes unblinking within their hoods. More moved in behind them and from other directions.

A claw clasped his shoulder. Wheeling, Brian found himself looking into huge, cold, bloodred eyes. He tried to break free but couldn't.

The thing that used to be Declan mac Coul had him.

THIRTY-EIGHT

The trio of saber-toothed frogs roared as they closed in on Doc, Wren, and Bartlett. Their skins were slick and shiny with river water.

Doc shifted gracefully into a relaxed battle posture. Wren removed an egg-shaped vial from a pocket on her utility vest. Phineas Bartlett assumed a fencer's stance, sword cane raised before him.

The saber-toothed monsters each chose separate prey. They leaped before their roars were finished, flying through the air with astonishing swiftness for beasts so large.

Doc dropped into a crouch, locking his fists together, then lunged up under his attacker as it dropped toward him, driving the fists straight into the gelatinous flesh of its belly.

The impact rattled the man of brawn's skeleton, but the sheer might of his legs and body channeled through his arms into the frog's body as if it had dropped on a steel post, stopping its pounce and flipping it over onto its back.

The creature lay quivering, stunned. A quick, hard jab just behind its skull put its lights out completely.

Wren snapped open her egg-shaped vial, hurling its contents at the snout of the frog coming at her, then rolled out of reach.

The thing landed and started thrashing on the ground, slapping its claws at its fanged froggish face, trying to get away from the powder coating its snout.

Itching powder.

Agonizingly intense itching powder.

Wren picked up a rock and cracked the thing on the top of its head, hard. The full dynamic force of her weight in the blow knocked it cold.

As his opponent flew at him, Phineas Bartlett took two jumps backward, just out of range. The snarling creature landed in front of him and Bartlett executed a perfect lunge, driving his sword dead center into its brow. Its eyes rolled, and the saber-toothed frog slumped, exhaling its last breath in a ghastly wheeze.

Doc motioned for the other two to gather close. They scrutinized their surroundings for signs of further attack, but there were none. "Seems that was all of them," Doc said. "For the moment, anyway."

He bent to examine the beast he'd knocked out.

"Incredible," he said. "It's as if all ecological niches in this region are filled by frogs."

Phineas Bartlett sheathed his sword, making it a cane once more. "Would I be safe in assuming such a thing is highly improbable?"

Doc chuckled. "To say the least. Something's going on here besides basic evolution. There's a sophisticated mind behind these creatures."

"Another mad scientist?" Wren asked.

"Could be," her dad said. "Someone highly skilled in genetic manipulation, with a deep neurotic identification with frogs. Then again, it could be some sort of dark magic."

"Another evil wizard," Wren said.

"Perhaps. Whoever it is, I think we're getting close. We'll find our answers soon." He squeezed her shoulder. "And we'll find your brother, Grandpa, and Declan."

Then Doc's expression hardened, and he quick-drew his gun. A horde of dark shapes dropped from the thick tree limbs above.

MAN-FROGS. At least fifty of them, probably more.

THIRTY-NINE

"I can't say I like these odds," Phineas Bartlett said. His sword-cane blade was bared once again.

"Me neither," Wren said. Like her dad, she had her pistol drawn.

They were surrounded. The man-frogs stared at the humans with their huge globular eyes, filling the jungle with excited croaks and ribbits.

"They're not here to attack us," Doc said, "or they'd have done it already. They're here to halt our progress or to take us captive."

Several tense minutes passed, with Doc and the others remaining on guard, just in case an attack *did* come.

The man-frogs seemed to be waiting for something. They stared and shuffled their webbed feet and croaked. The croaks had been haphazard, the chaotic voice of a crowd, but as the minutes crawled past, a change washed over the frogs. They slowly began to croak in unison. Dozens of deep amphibian calls merged into one loud, rhythmic rumble . . . **croak** . . . **croak** . . . **CROAK** . . .

Then the croaks themselves changed, warping into a word, a single word croaked forth from many voices.

COME . . . COME . . . COME . . . COME . . .

The man-frogs all raised one claw and pointed across the river. Those between the humans and the river moved to the sides, opening a channel to it, some of them hopping into the water to continue the channel to the far bank.

"Well," Wren said, "at least this way we'll get where we're going faster than we would have by tracking."

"Yes," Doc Wilde said. "Getting captured can have its benefits."

The humans allowed themselves to be herded across the river, then onward. The bizarre procession moved mile after mile through the jungle. The light dimmed even further as night covered them, and Doc brought out a bright light stick so they could see. The hills grew more jagged and steep as they drew nearer to the Andes.

Well after midnight, they came to the sheer volcanic ridges of the mountains, and there they reached their destination: the monstrous cave they feared had swallowed Grandpa Wilde.

FORTY

The company of man-frogs stood silently as Doc, Wren, and Bartlett approached the beastly stone frog.

The cave mouth was a spectacular sight. Intricately carved from the rock of the mountain, its dark surface was mottled green and brown with lichens and moss. It was enormous, at least sixteen feet high at its peak. Brawny vines and roots spilled past its sides, making it look as if it were emerging threateningly from a jungle thicket.

Its spidery claws seemed ready to tear into flesh, its gaping shark-toothed maw ready to swallow its prey whole.

"I'm glad this isn't *my* house," Wren said.

"'Great holes secretly are digged where earth's pores ought to suffice,'" Bartlett quoted, "'and things have learnt to walk that ought to crawl.'"

"H. P. Lovecraft?" Wren asked.

Bartlett nodded, staring soberly at the terrible amphibian visage.

It occurred to Wren that though they'd encountered several bizarre frog mutations, they hadn't encountered any that looked like *this*. If this was a representation of an actual beast, she wondered if it was life size. It'd be cool to see a thing like that. From a distance.

The silent man-frogs began to vocalize again, muttered croaks this time morphing into:

"IN . . . IN . . . IN . . . IN . . ."

FORTY-ONE

It was clammy within the cave, and a faint breeze blew toward the exit. A handful of man-frogs followed them from outside, keeping about ten feet behind, clearly serving as guards.

The passage was weakly lit by a luminous fungus lightly coating its walls, about as effective as if the three of them were each carrying a single lit birthday candle. It was a light made for large eyes used to a subterranean world.

Doc relit his light stick, and they marched deeper underground.

Ahead, a figure stood in the center of the tunnel. As they neared, they saw it wore a crimson robe rather than green like the others. The color was like the red of a poison arrow frog.

Doc brought them to a halt about ten feet away from the creature, and the three humans waited.

"*Hola*, Dr. Wilde!" the figure exclaimed. "Once more, you are my guests!"

The figure flipped back his red hood, revealing the mustachioed smile of Don Rodrigo Gongoro.

"Welcome to the *true* capital of Hidalgo, my friends."

"I like the other capital better," Wren said.

Doc Wilde's jaw was set and his eyes ablaze, but his stance remained calm. This was not the time for a fight. "Where's my father, Gongoro?" he asked.

"Oh, you shall find that out *muy pronto*. But now, my schedule is very full. Big things are happening today!"

Don Rodrigo gestured to another figure deeper in the tunnel; it moved to his side. It too wore a red robe but was very much a man-frog.

Don Rodrigo bowed. "We shall all see each other again soon, my friends." And with that, he vanished down the tunnel.

"Greeting," the man-frog said. Its voice was guttural and inhuman but clear.

"Hello," Doc Wilde replied.

"You will follow," it said. It turned its back to them and started walking, its flipper feet smacking lightly on the stone floor.

They walked deeper into the mountain. The cave twisted onward, descending, with only a few other caves intersecting. Wren realized it was warmer than it had been when they entered. "Why is it getting warmer?" she asked.

"This range is made up of volcanoes, so there's a good deal of volcanic heat," her dad replied. "It makes sense that cold-blooded creatures would want a warm nest."

Soon, the cave opened into a large, rounded chamber, its far half a pool of water. Hanging from pegs in the walls were dozens of robes, all old and worn, riddled with dark currents of mold. The tunnel behind seemed to be the only exit.

Two dark heads broke the water's surface, and two naked man-frogs splashed out and stood at the red-robed figure's side. Without clothes, the man-frogs were among the ickiest things Wren had ever seen.

Their guide turned to face them. "Weapons and vests here," it croaked.

Wren and Bartlett looked to Doc, ready to follow his lead.

Doc Wilde looked thoughtful. "Are we going under-water?"

"Under this water," the red-robed guide said.

"Then we need one thing from our vests to make sure we don't drown," Doc told it.

"One thing," it told him.

The Wildes produced three small rebreather mouthpieces, handing one to Bartlett. Doc and Wren surrendered their vests and holsters to the dripping man-frogs from the pool.

Phineas Bartlett glared at the creatures, then stiffly handed over his sword cane.

The red-robed guide hung its robe with the others. "Follow," it commanded, hopping into the water and sinking away.

Biting their rebreathers, the humans followed.

FORTY-TWO

The water was warm, like a comfortable bath, and soft currents played with their hair and clothing as they swam. The man-frog frog-kicked his way forward swiftly, almost too fast for them to keep up with.

They were in a watery void: they could see no walls and no bottom. The stone ceiling loomed above like a coffin lid.

Wren had scary thoughts of losing sight of their guide, getting turned the wrong way down here, and never finding their way back to a world of air . . .

What if this was just an ingenious trap designed to lure enemies to their watery dooms?

She was absolutely *treasuring* her rebreather right now, which used her dad's nanotech to draw dissolved oxygen from the water, allowing hours of submerged breathing.

More scary thoughts arose as she sensed large dark shapes flashing past nearby. More man-frogs? Or worse? Probably worse.

Suddenly, the guide sliced upward, surfacing in another tunnel. They followed it back onto solid stone, pocketing their rebreathers. As in the previous chamber, an array of robes hung here, and the guide donned a moldy crimson one identical to what it had left behind.

Doc Wilde wore a half smile as their guide led them down the tunnel. "What an incredible place," he said quietly. "I bet the entire complex is a labyrinth with its sections connected only through a deep subterranean lake. An attacking force would either have to find its way through the lake—into the narrow tunnels of the labyrinth, where they could easily be swarmed as they tried to leave the water—or blast their way through solid volcanic stone hundreds of feet thick. Ingenious."

"The perfect fortress," Phineas Bartlett agreed.

It was also a perfect prison, Wren thought. They had gotten in easily enough, but that didn't mean it'd be easy getting out.

The tunnel split in two, and their guide took them leftward. A short distance later, there was a three-tunnel fork, and they went straight. From there, they crossed many intersections, zigzagging the deep core of the mountain. Most people would have quickly lost all sense of where they were and where they had been, but with her ingrained mental discipline, Wren systematically built a three-dimensional map of their progress in her memory as they went.

One passage spiraled up several hundred feet. At the top, they found the intersection of five more tunnels and headed down one.

That tunnel ended at an archway into a round chamber. Half a dozen man-frogs in green robes stood sentry. Their guide pointed a claw through the arch and stood aside.

"In," it croaked, and in they went.

Before they could react to what waited inside, a huge slab of stone crashed down behind them, **blocking the only exit.**

FORTY-THREE

Oddly, the chamber in which they were now trapped was furnished with a line of bunk beds, a wooden table, and several chairs. A bowl of fruit sat on the table.

Seated at the table, gaming with a very worn deck of cards, were Grandpa Wilde and Brian.

"DAD!" Brian leaped to his feet and ran to his father. Doc Wilde crouched and caught him in his strong arms.

"I knew you'd find us," Brian said.

"Where's Declan?" Doc asked.

"Somewhere in the mountain," Brian said. "But he's not quite himself . . . "

Doc nodded. "He's being controlled by or through the emerald frog, isn't he?"

Brian's eyes widened. "Yeah . . . but how . . . ?"

"Your tracks. I could tell that no one was with either of you and that you were stealthily following him. Since Declan's not prone to spontaneous nocturnal jungle-wandering and the frog was missing, I figured it had to be something like that."

Grandpa Wilde smiled warmly and crossed to them. He tousled Wren's hair and clapped a strong hand on Doc's shoulder. "You kids okay?" he asked.

Doc hugged his father. "We're fine. It's been quite an adventure. These frog creatures are fascinating."

"Yes indeed," Grandpa said.

To look at Clark Wilde, Jr., was to see without doubt that he was Doc's father. He looked very much like Doc, only a few decades older: he appeared about sixty but was actually ninety-nine years old.

The kids had seen pictures of him from the 1930s, his hair in a crisp, no-fuss crew cut and his face stern. According to Grandma Pat, he'd been mostly humorless, socially awkward, very stolid, and all about "The Mission," which was how he referred to the crimebusting life he and his aides led then. According to Grandpa, over the years Pat had taught him to smile, then to laugh, then to play. Now his once-golden hair was snow white and worn in a longish, somewhat wild style, looking perpetually windblown.

Amazingly, he still possessed the massive physique he'd had in his youth; his limbs still rippled with power.

The resemblance between Grandpa Wilde and Doc was reinforced by the fact they were dressed exactly alike. Grandpa Wilde's shirt even hung in tatters, just as Doc's did.

"It'll be time to get out of here and defeat some evil soon," Grandpa Wilde said. "So have a seat; I'll fill you in on the parts of the story that you don't know."

They all sat at the table. Wren grabbed a banana from the bowl to eat while she listened.

"As you likely know, I was at Harvard giving a speech about dark matter," Grandpa said. "There I met a brilliant graduate student, Carlos Gongoro, who told me of a place in Hidalgo he believed was an ancient gateway into a dark matter universe. He sketched the frog cave, and I recognized the design: it was the spitting image of an emerald frog I took from the criminal mastermind Large Mouth Benny when he tried to take over the world back in '48.

"Carlos acted surprised, though it's now clear his froggy fraternity knew I had the piece somewhere all along. I retrieved it from our secret warehouse, then flew us to Verde Grande in my speed plane. There, Carlos's uncle, Don Rodrigo, Hidalgo's *caudillo*, proved a gracious host, but I could tell his troops were spying on me."

"We can relate," Brian said.

Grandpa looked thoughtful. "I liked Carlos Gongoro, but everything he said became suspect, so I hid the emerald frog in one of my plane's secret caches before we left town.

"Carlos and I flew north as far as we could, then landed on a river and backpacked the rest of the way in. As we got closer, the jungle started to get weird."

"Land of Bizarro Frogs," Wren said.

Grandpa chuckled. "Exactly. When we reached the cave, I was amazed at how precisely the carving resembled the emerald frog.

"I handed Carlos my camera, asking him to get a good shot as I stood in the cave. Carlos laughed and took the picture.

"Then a horde of frog-men swarmed us. Carlos grinned and told me not to worry, that we were perfectly safe and all would be explained.

"They brought me through tunnels wet and dry to an actual *office*. At the desk sat Don Rodrigo Gongoro.

"What he told me was astonishing."

FORTY-FOUR

Don Rodrigo Gongoro spun Grandpa Wilde a tale terrifying and dark, of indescribable horrors and eldritch mysteries . . .

A tale of shadows out of time and colors out of space . . .

A tale of whispery croaks from the darkness . . .

It was a terrible tale, and, if true, it proved the elder Wilde's theories: there *were* dark matter universes and it *was* possible to travel to them. It just might not be a good idea.

Some of these outside realms are ruled by ancient powers, elder gods far older than our earth, perhaps older than our universe itself. And these powers don't exactly have our best interests at heart.

In one of the madder darknesses, one such god dwelled, wanting very much to clamber out of its black waters onto our lily pad. It took the form of a great and terrible frog with long, spidery claws and sharklike rows of dagger teeth.

A frog as big as a universe. Bigger, even. Uncountable aeons ago, it had swallowed its own universe. To look into its maw was to see the slowing swirl of dying galaxies, the light of their stars winking out as the frog digested time itself.

This dark god's name was Frogon.

For untold ages, Frogon scratched at the membranes of different realities, and millennia ago its efforts opened holes into our world. The holes were far too small for Frogon to hop through, but it peeked and watched and plotted.

Having consumed its own universe, it wanted to consume ours.

Emanations of Frogon's arcane power radiated from these holes, affecting living things nearby. In a sense, the corrupt god did us a favor: when it first cast its bulging gaze upon the earth, all life swam in thundering seas. Frogon's power warped the forms of the primitive creatures within its radius, bringing them forth onto the jagged shores of primeval time. Thus, amphibians were born.

Many amphibians slithered and hopped out of the earthly realms of Frogon; outside its influence, under the sway of nature, they evolved further, into dinosaurs, reptiles, birds, mammals . . . ultimately, into us.

In the areas close to the dimensional holes, life

evolved as well. But as the Wildes had seen, all animal life in those places consisted entirely of mutated frogs.

Sometimes a creature from outside Frogon's lands wandered into them. If it remained and survived, it gradually transmogrified into some froggy shape.

Thus, when humans came to these regions, they changed. They became the man-frogs, who are called "Leap Ones."

There were Leap Ones before men tilled the soil, kept livestock, built civilizations.

The Leap Ones' goal is to rip the dark one's peepholes asunder, to let Frogon into this universe.

The closest they ever came was when a Leap One mystic discovered a way to combine dark energies from Frogon and from our world to craft a key to open a way between universes: the emerald frog. Before he could use that key, he was slain by a wild-haired barbarian from Sumeria. The mystic took his secrets to the grave; the frog vanished into the mists of antiquity (until the villain Large Mouth Benny somehow got his mitts on it, only to have his plots foiled by Grandpa Wilde).

Such was the tale told by Don Rodrigo Gongoro, *caudillo* of Hidalgo, who also proclaimed that he occupied a much more sacred post: high priest of the Temple of Frogon.

FORTY-FIVE

"Don Rodrigo thought I'd unwittingly delivered the emerald frog to him," Grandpa Wilde said. "With it, he planned to open the doorway into the dark universe and let Frogon in."

"What'd he do when he found out you didn't have it?" Brian asked.

"He said I was to die anyway, but if I didn't point them to the frog, I'd suffer a 'truly horrible death.'"

"But why tell you all that if he was just going to kill you?" Wren asked.

"Villains always do that kind of thing," Brian said. "It's their way of bragging."

Grandpa nodded, smiling, then continued. "My instincts about Carlos had been dead-on: he *was* a decent guy. He lied to get me here, but I think he imagined that after hearing the truth, I'd help them commune with their great benevolent god. He thought they were *good guys*. But when the talk turned to murdering me, Carlos was clearly shocked.

"Don Rodrigo ordered his amphibian goons to grab me, and Carlos jumped in front of them, demanding his uncle call them off. Don Rodrigo screamed that Carlos was not to question him and should stand aside.

"Carlos didn't move. I told him it was all right and convinced him to step away. Then the Leap Ones dragged me off and threw me in here."

"I assume Carlos sent us the frog and the picture of you," Doc Wilde said to his father.

"Yes. As I was brought to this room, we had a whispered talk. I told him where the emerald frog was hidden on my plane, and how to activate the homing computer. A huge risk, but that's the kind Wildes like best, eh? I haven't seen him since. I hope the boy's okay."

"Let us hope Don Rodrigo didn't realize the depth of Carlos's misgivings," Phineas Bartlett said.

There was a loud scrape as the stone rose from the doorway, then a young Hidalgan was shoved into the room. The stone smashed back down just behind him, and he stumbled to his hands and knees. His clothes were torn, his face bruised.

"Senor Wilde," he said, "I am so sorry."

Grandpa rushed to help him to his feet. "No, Carlos, you did the right thing. Thank you."

Carlos shook his head. "I was caught trying to stop my uncle's plans, and now he has promised my death. But that doesn't matter! He's going to open the portal to let Frogon through . . .

. . . our universe is doomed!"

FORTY-SIX

"The ritual is beginning," Carlos told the Wildes. "The portal will open in less than an hour."

"Then we'd best get out of this cell now," Doc said.

Grandpa Wilde nodded, returning to the table to pocket the cards he and Brian had been playing with.

They faced the huge rock slab that blocked the only exit from the room.

Larger than the archway, the slab had fallen into place; no visible mechanism controlled its movement. No cables, no tracks, no levers or gears . . . nothing to manipulate. The great stone was inside the room, its bulk tight against the wall around the opening. Moving it seemed as likely as lifting an elephant over your head.

"How are we going to get through *that*?" Wren asked.

"The old-fashioned way," Doc said. "We're going to push it."

The kids nodded. If Dad said they could do it, he knew they could.

"Hmm," Grandpa said, eyeing the stone. "It won't be easy. It'll take all of us, I think."

"Yes," Doc Wilde said. "Let's move."

Pointing out a minuscule leftward slant he'd noted in the floor, Doc gathered them to the right side of the block. It was thick enough for three men to stand facing it side by side, and that was what they did: Doc stood closest to the wall, Grandpa at the inner edge, with Phineas Bartlett between them.

Carlos Gongoro was a good deal shorter than them; Doc had Carlos stand in front of him, below his arms. Brian and Wren took places in front of Grandpa Wilde and Bartlett respectively.

"Okay . . . *focus*," Doc Wilde said.

Grandpa, Bartlett, and the kids knew he was giving a very specific command. To them, focus was much more than simple mental concentration: it was a spiritual exercise rooted in their martial arts training. They relaxed their muscles and deepened their breathing. Their thoughts turned inward, their awareness shifting to another state. And they sensed the flow of chi, the life force that flows through all things, as it flowed through them, forming a circuit of energy between where their feet touched the floor and where their hands pressed the slab.

This came so naturally after years of meditative practice that it was done within seconds. Carlos had no notion of what they'd done but all the same suddenly felt a shimmering tension in the air, so strong he heard a strange trilling buzz in his inner ear.

Doc Wilde said, purely for Carlos's sake; the Wildes and Bartlett were so in tune they breathed in unison and knew wordlessly when to act.

Six pairs of feet pressed the stone floor. Six pairs of hands pushed the stone slab.

Muscles tightened, but not as much as you'd think: most of the force came from the channeled chi energy, which gave them far more strength than muscle alone could have.

Gravity pulled at the tons of stone. Friction against the floor resisted motion; in spite of their effort, the slab would not move.

Until it did.

The stone slipped forward a fraction of an inch. Inertia broken, it rode the channeled chi and the pressure of their hands in a smooth slide toward the doorway's left.

The opening appeared, first an inch, then three inches, then ten . . .

They pushed. The opening gaped wide enough for a broad-chested man to slip through.

Carlos shoved, slick with sweat. Realizing the others had stopped, he turned and slumped against the slab, dizzy with the effort but grinning at the astonishing feat they'd just performed.

Suddenly, a Leap One guard appeared in the opening, croaking angrily.

Doc struck, his arm swifter than a cobra. There was a **THUNK**, and he dragged the now-unconscious man-frog into the room. The golden adventurer disappeared through the gap; by the time the others stepped out, he was standing over two more immobilized guards.

Three others leaped toward him.

Brian and Wren charged together, tackling one. They spilled in a jumble on the corridor floor. Brian grabbed the Leap One's arms, grappling with it as Wren scrambled up and struck a pressure point in its neck, a point that would render a person unconscious. Fortunately, the Leap One's anatomy was close enough to its original human form, and it slumped to the cave floor.

Doc whirled, grabbing one of the creatures in the air just as Grandpa Wilde did the same with the remaining one, and they stepped toward each other, slamming the Leap Ones' heads together. The man-frogs dropped to the ground like wet scarecrows.

"Do you know where they took our gear?" Doc asked Carlos.

The Hidalgan nodded. "Yes, the storage sector. But there are hundreds of Leap Ones within the mountain . . . "

"Take us," Doc Wilde commanded.

FORTY-SEVEN

They ran down the tunnel, not seeing any Leap Ones until they reached the five-way intersection. There, they surprised a pair of guards and left them crumpled on the floor, then charged down the long spiral passageway.

At the end of the spiral, Carlos led them along a different route than the one they'd originally traveled. They **ZIGGED** and *ZAGGED* and **SPIRALED** through the volcanic stone, encountering no more members of the Cult of Frogon along the way.

"Where are all the frog guys?" Brian asked.

"They must be gathering in the temple for the ritual," Carlos answered.

Finally, at a corridor's end, they reached one of the pools.

Wren and Bartlett bit onto their breathers. Doc let Brian use his and would hold his breath, as would Grandpa and Carlos.

"It won't be a problem," the young Hidalgan said, "I have swum this lake many times."

Again they descended into liquid darkness . . .

They stayed close together. It would be terrible to get out of one another's sight out in these black depths, to drift away to a stygian death.

Ahead, Wren spotted the sloshing paleness of an opening, another of the pools; Carlos led them that way.

They surfaced, scanning the chamber around them for threats but found none.

They paddled toward the rock-ledge shore.

Wren reached it, relieved as she got her hands on solid stone and heaved her weight up—

Then, under the water, something heavy bumped her. Several muscular *things* twisted around her legs. She screamed,

"DAD!"

and her rebreather fell to the stone as she was yanked back into the watery dark.

FORTY-EIGHT

Doc grabbed Wren's rebreather from the pool's edge and tossed it to Grandpa Wilde as both men dove after the girl.

Brian was right behind them, kicking toward her, aware of Bartlett and Carlos splashing in nearby. Wren was just a few feet away—

No, she was already gone.

Doc and Grandpa speared downward, vanishing in the murk.

Brian circled above, desperately watching for motion, listening for sounds of submerged struggle, sensing variations in the currents with the water's flow over his skin, through his hair.

Nothing.

He spiraled deeper, not seeing his dad, not sensing anything of his sister or her unknown attacker.

It would be easy to lose the pool opening if he went too far or too deep.

Brian kicked back up, joining the others. They swam in quick, expanding circles underwater . . .

Nothing.

His father, who was without a rebreather, shot to the surface for air, then knifed again into darkness. Doc and Carlos breached the pool's surface many times, gasping for air, immediately diving again. Again and again, for a long time, while Brian and the others with rebreathers stayed submerged, thrashing the darkness without luck.

Wren was gone.

FORTY-NINE

Slimy tentacles squeezed Wren's legs as the monster towed her through the water at amazing speed.

Spun and twisted in myriad directions, she lost all sense of direction in the dark water. All she knew was the thing had her tightly, it was taking her somewhere, and she was running out of air.

She stopped thrashing. It wasn't working, and the exertion burned oxygen. She had to *think*, not fight. And she had to think *fast*.

Muscles relaxed, she used the mental skills her dad taught her to slow her heart, her entire metabolism, and thus the rate her body burned oxygen. Her mind flashed second by second through possible means of survival. But she had no weapons or gear, and she couldn't overpower the thing. She sensed they were getting deeper and deeper, and her lungs were starting to burn.

But she knew that every animal in Frogon's jungle was some weird variety of frog, and frogs breathe *air*.

Except, of course, when they were babies. Tadpoles

had gills, like fish. And there were salamanders like the siren and mud puppy, which were strictly aquatic and had gills . . . but if this thing was like all Frogon's other creatures, it wasn't a salamander, it wasn't just an amphibian of *some* sort, it was, indeed, a **FROG.**

If so, it could probably hold its breath a long time, much longer than her. But it *would* need air; it *would* have lungs.

It was all she could come up with. Thinking it through took just under eighteen seconds.

The current world record for *actual* breath-holding, without preparing by breathing pure oxygen for dozens of minutes, was right around nine minutes; thanks to physical and mental training she'd had since she was a baby, under optimal conditions Wren could hold hers for about five max (her dad, who was unconcerned about world record glory and didn't boast, could do nearly twelve!).

These weren't optimal conditions. The thing yanked her underwater in midgasp, and she'd burned some air in the short tussle before relaxing. She had two, maybe three minutes before her lungs got their way and took a deep breath, not a great idea underwater.

Hopefully, this would work.

She couldn't see at all in the absolute darkness. Tentatively, she arched her body forward, toward the creature, reaching with both hands. Hoping not to find one of those gaping maws of sharp teeth.

Fingertips found slimy skin.

She slipped her hands over what was clearly the thing's head; she could feel the solidness of its skull inside. She found the rubbery line of its closed lips (which thankfully remained closed), and it twitched. She found its nostrils, the edges of its bulging eyes . . .

Frog. Tentacled weird mutant frog. But **frog.**

With sudden force, Wren embraced the monster, arms locking behind its skull. Simultaneously, she pulled her body into a fetal curl, knees up in front of her. She squeezed tightly, hugging the creature to her, then drove her knees into its belly with all her focused strength.

The unseen monster grunted hugely, a sound like a giant, painful burp. Hope flared in Wren's heart as she heard a great burst of bubbles erupt from its mouth. She slammed her knees into it again and again.

The thing thrashed; she felt small webbed feet slap feebly at her sides, but all its strength seemed to be in its tentacles.

Her lungs were *on fire*.

The monster's zoom through the water had stopped with the first painful hug. But as it lost its air, it panicked.

Tentacles loosened, and the beast swam away, or tried to. Wren, knowing she couldn't be left here in the black depths and still find her way to air in time, held the embrace with all her strength, though she let her legs hang loose so they wouldn't impede the beast's progress.

They surged through the water. Wren clenched her jaws so hard to keep from breathing that her teeth hurt. Her mind was starting to spin; she'd either black out and drown or just drown if they didn't reach air *soon*.

Then they were splashing. They'd surfaced. Somewhere. The frog thing's gasps were rough and sputtering. Wren let go of the monster and kicked away, feeling for some sort of shore.

She found a sloshing slope of grating volcanic sand and dragged her torso from the water, convulsively breathing in the moist warm air.

The sputtering behind her ceased and she heard a small splash as the creature submerged. She rolled over, sitting up in the shallow water, and jerked her legs in, sliding backward.

She was *not* letting that thing grab her again.

Nothing happened. Maybe the beast had decided she was too much trouble.

Wren sat in the darkness and wondered what to do.

FIFTY

Dr. Spartacus Wilde loved nothing in this world or any other as much as he loved his kids. This was obvious to anyone who knew him for at least a minute or two. So Brian knew his father's heart was breaking as he told Carlos to lead them onward, into the labyrinth . . . away from the pool in which Wren vanished.

Brian felt like his soul itself was torn.

But all they could do was go on. Don Rodrigo Gongoro and the Leap One priests would soon perform the ritual opening this universe to the one within Frogon, and the dark elder god would swallow all of earth, all of space, all of time in the plane of existence in which they dwelled.

If they didn't stop Don Rodrigo, all of creation was doomed.

After they saved the universe, they could look for Wren.

Through the dim tunnels they raced until they reached the chamber where their gear was stored.

They encountered no resistance. The entire horde of Leap Ones—less those who'd been guarding them—were apparently gathered en masse for the eldritch ceremony. That was a good thing now, but it also meant there would be an amphibious mob to deal with when they got to the temple.

All their gear was where Carlos said it would be, including Grandpa Wilde's. The three Wildes geared up, Brian donning Wren's holster and vest, which just fit with a few quick adjustments.

Phineas Bartlett secured his shoulder holster, then picked up his sword cane with a serene smile.

"We must hurry," Carlos Gongoro said.

"Yes," Brian agreed, his golden eyes blazing. All he could think of was getting this universe-threatening nonsense out of the way so he could look for his sister. She was as wily and smart as any of the Wildes—but he was still worried.

Carlos guided them onward through the volcanic maze. This way, that way, up, down, over to another pool.

"We have to swim again," Carlos said. Doc nodded. None of them said anything, but all were thinking of Wren.

Back into the warm, black water . . .

Four times, Carlos surfaced them in pools, but only for a moment's rest before they dove again.

Fortunately, Carlos possessed an unerring ability to negotiate the confusing paths of this subterranean fortress. Though he didn't know it, it came to him because deep in his DNA and his soul, he'd begun the transmogrification that ultimately would make him a Leap One. The minds of the Leap Ones resonated with one another and with their dark god like a low-grade hive mind. Within Frogon's realm, Leap Ones could never be lost.

Finally, they reached a shaft in the ceiling slightly wider than a trash can lid, rising vertically into the stone. They bobbed one by one into the shaft, finding its walls carved into ringed segments they could climb like a ladder.

The shaft rose about a hundred feet, opening into a large chamber. The floor was carpeted in thick, soft moss, which to the Wildes' trained eyes showed signs of many webbed feet. A deep bass rumble vibrated the stone, and after a moment, Brian realized it was the chanting of a *lot* of Leap Ones.

"We are nearly there," Carlos told them. "The entrance is down that tunnel, but it would take us right into the gathering. Come up this way; there's a good place to see what's going on."

They followed him up a slanting corridor. The floor moss disappeared. The chanting faded. A couple of turns and they ascended one of the spiral tunnels. At the top, they could hear the chanting again.

A narrow side corridor led to their destination: a high ledge overlooking the temple.

The temple was vast, about the size of two sports arenas. A huge pool at the center opened into the dark waters of the subterranean lake. Thousands of Leap Ones crowded the space right to the edge of the pool, bobbing and chanting in a spiritual frenzy. Their voices echoed in an uneven roar, rising and falling like waves in a storm.

Four sets of stone stairs arched from the sides of the pool, merging into a flat disk of stone serving as a ceremonial platform. Atop it stood Don Rodrigo Gongoro and three Leap Ones, all wearing the red robes of Frogon's high priests, all on their knees bowing at the feet of a horrible figure:

DECLAN MAC COUL.

FIFTY-ONE

Darkness and wet stone. That was Wren's world now. The pool where she and the weird tentacled mutant frog had parted was in a low-ceilinged blister cave, a bubble trapped in cooling lava long ago. She'd been extremely lucky: most such caves are isolated cavities in the volcanic rock, unconnected to other passages. If that had been the case, she'd have been entombed in mountain stone, with no exit possible but the unfathomable black waters she'd just escaped.

Fortunately, a few moments of carefully feeling around revealed that the small cave was connected to a passageway like a leaf on a stem. The passage was a tight lava tube, cracked by earthquakes, and once again Wren's small size was an asset. She crept into the tunnel, going left. There was no way to know if it was the direction she should go, how long the tunnel was, or if it would remain spacious enough for her.

Or if it even led anywhere. Unlike the Leap Ones' caves, here there was no phosphorescent fungus to share its meek glow. The darkness was absolute. Navigating the tube wasn't an issue, there was only forward and back, but Wren dreaded the possibility of reaching a dead end, her only option to crawl *backward* the way she'd come.

She banished thoughts she might never get out of here. That sort of thinking created limits in a person's mind: blocks to imagination, loss of important memory, deadening of awareness. *In any situation,* her dad advised, *don't dwell on what you can't do, look for things that you can.*

Her progress was slow. She had to crawl, at some points even drag forward on her belly. The stone loomed heavily all around her; it banged her head, scraped her back, and cut her hands. It tore her shirt and wore the knees from her pants. The humid air proved too warm, and she became sticky with sweat within her already-damp clothes.

Then she got a break. The tunnel suddenly expanded: the cramped walls and ceiling veered out of reach, and the bottom dropped away. She was relieved to discover that the floor ahead had only dropped about a foot. She edged out, sensing only open space around her, and stood, grateful to be vertical again. She stood on tiptoe, reaching straight up, and didn't touch the ceiling. This was either a cavern or the small lava tube had converged with a larger passage.

Feeling like she'd been beaten with mallets, she stretched to limber up and uncramp her muscles. But she couldn't pause for long; she had to find her dad and the others. They were headed into incredible danger. They'd need her help.

Something terrible might happen.

Or things would go great, and she'd miss all the fun.

FIFTY-TWO

Declan was barely recognizable, so far had the eldritch radiation of the emerald frog taken him, becoming far more monstrous than the other man-frogs. His eyes were gigantic bloodred orbs, his body was bloated out of human shape, skin dark green mottled brown, and his mouth was a grinning maw of needle teeth. He was well on his way to becoming the fleshly embodiment of the frog god on earth.

Atop his head, the emerald frog shone like the shimmering reflection of a hot noon sun on green swamp water. Looking directly at him, even at this distance, left an afterimage burning in Brian's eyes.

"I regret having to say this," Phineas Bartlett whispered, "but I preferred him the other way."

No reply was needed; they all agreed. Declan's role in the proceedings, and his altered condition, were worrisome. They'd have to get past the army of Leap Ones, face whatever dark powers Declan and Don Rodrigo might muster, grab Declan (who wasn't likely to come along willingly), find Wren, then escape the perplexing labyrinth of the mountain itself.

On the platform, Declan croaked an order and the high priests at his feet rose. They started a hopping dance that was picked up by the Leap One horde surrounding them. All bobbed in sync, up, down, up, down, up, down, creating a surreal accordion effect.

The emerald frog throbbed brighter with each surge.

"Time is short," Carlos whispered.

Doc nodded. Brian watched him, waiting for his dad to give them their cues, lead them into battle, execute some mind-boggling plan. Brian did a quick inventory of all the gear they had while at the same time scanning the vast space of the temple for anything that might be useful. That was what his dad would be doing, Brian hoped with better results, because he himself was coming up with zip. It felt like a situation with *no* options available, and Brian didn't like the feeling. It settled in his gut like a quart of bad milk.

His fear for Wren made it far worse.

Below the platform, the dark water of the large pool began to surge in time with the chants, the dance, the pulsing emerald light. It sloshed from rim to center like the ripples of an enormous splash, only in reverse.

"Dad . . . ?" Brian said, his voice competing with all the noise. "What are we going to do?"

Doc Wilde's usually cheerful face was stone. His reply was like an icy claw on Brian's soul.

"I don't know, son. I don't know."

FIFTY-THREE

There are few places on earth as deadly as a cave with no light. Caves are fractured labyrinths without plan, without predictable sizes or lengths or depths. The ground underfoot can suddenly vanish over a sheer cliff or down a gaping shaft plummeting thousands of feet. Death waits in the utter darkness, maybe yards, maybe feet, maybe just inches ahead. Even when properly equipped and carrying light, trained spelunkers know to go slowly, carefully, because the buried ways of the earth are innately unfriendly and a misstep can be your last step.

Faced with the nightmarish mystery of the dark cavern ahead, Wren paused, all of that clear in her mind. Then she took a deep breath and ran.

She went faster than a jog, but not quite as fast as a sprint. The smack of her boots on stone was slight, as Wren was not only tiny and light but like all the Wildes moved with a trained grace that made little sound.

When she reached a sudden drop in the ceiling

height, she ducked just in time. When the tunnel turned abruptly, she veered appropriately to keep to the path. And when a bottomless hole gaped ahead, waiting to swallow her for eternity, Wren leaped across, landing in a springy crouch on the far side.

She had no light, no equipment to help make her way through the abysmal black. She had no familiarity with her surroundings. It should have been impossible for her to pass so swiftly, so surely, through these perilous depths, and yet she did.

She couldn't use her exceptional eyesight, so she used her mouth and her ears. Just like a bat.

A bat using sonar emits a steady series of sounds that return to the ears as minute echoes. These echoes form sonic shapes, images of sound, in the brain, which the creature uses to "see" the world around it.

As Wren ran through the caves, she used human echolocation, which her dad had trained her and her brother in since birth. She made rapid clicking noises in her throat, and her sharp ears caught their returning echoes, allowing her to sense the size and shape and distance of surfaces and objects in the darkness engulfing her.

Though far more primitive than the sonar of a creature that has naturally evolved sonar (Wren's clicks came at about two per second while a dolphin's come at around nine hundred per second and a bat's at an even higher rate than that), this actually produced a "view" in the visual centers of her brain, and the effect for the young Wilde was like running through very dim light.

As Wren ran, she collected impressions beyond shape and location. The lava tube had indeed merged with a larger tube, but many others intersected this cave. She kept to the main course, following it as a lost hiker might follow a river, hoping it would eventually lead somewhere. Also, the fewer turns she made, the easier it would be to backtrack if necessary.

Occasionally, she heard *things* moving in neighboring caves, and once, she heard a deep grunt. It sounded like a warthog in a barrel, but she was sure it was some kind of **ribbit**.

The Leap Ones inhabited an intricate labyrinth within the mountain, but all around them must be a hive of these caves, full of creatures that hunted in darkness. Perhaps they scavenged scraps from the Leap Ones, or were the Leap Ones' pets, or even ate the Leap Ones.

Heart pounding, Wren ran through the blackness making her clicks, hoping they wouldn't draw the attention of something else out there that might, like her earlier attacker, want to eat *her*.

FIFTY-FOUR

The army of Leap Ones bobbed and chanted, their voices a terrible roar in the gigantic cavern temple. The monster that had once been Declan mac Coul paced the ceremonial platform, its clawed hands weaving mystical signs in the air, the emerald frog on its head flashing its furious light. Doc, Brian, and the others watched from their high ledge overlooking the amphibious horde.

The wide pool beneath the ceremonial platform surged toward its own center in slapping waves timed with each rising chant. At the center, as the shrinking ripples came together, a hole formed, and water poured in. The hole expanded slightly with each call from the Leap Ones.

The portal was opening.

Very soon, Frogon would break through.

Whatever Doc and his team were going to do, they needed to do it *now*.

Doc Wilde stood. He slipped two walnut-size grenades from pouches on his vest, taking one in each hand.

"Cover your eyes," he ordered. And activating the grenades, he threw them in separate directions over the Leap Ones.

He turned his back to the temple.

None of the Wildes or their companions were looking when the grenades went off high in the air, so they weren't affected by the twin supernovas of light the explosives released. Each brilliant burst was bright enough to temporarily blind even animals who lived in daylight, like humans. To creatures of murk and mire and shadow, the light was beyond blinding. It was a jet of fire in their eyes.

A shriek rose from thousands of amphibious throats, a sound so terrible our heroes had to cover their ears. The chant was broken, and the dance was stilled. The Leap Ones thrashed and stumbled, crashing into one another in a panic.

As the flash faded, Doc produced a rod-shaped pocket grapnel. He slammed one end into the stone wall by the ledge, and a hooked spike of titanium shot from it with such force it sank more than a foot into the rock.

Drawing the device back, Doc pointed its other end over the heads of Frogon's army and a second spike rocketed out, unreeling a thin titanium jumpline between it and the embedded spike.

Doc's aim was true: the second spike buried itself in the closest of the stairways arcing up to the platform.

"This way," he said, unreeling his own jump line from his belt buckle, hooking it to the taut wire of the grapnel, and leaping from the ledge.

He zipped over the terrified Leap Ones, unhooking himself and landing in a *ninjutsu* stance on the stairs.

Brian followed. He landed at his father's back, assuming an identical posture but facing downward, toward the churning sea of Leap Ones. Golden eyes intense, shirts hanging in shreds, father and son looked like reflections of each other.

Carlos rode piggyback as Grandpa Wilde flew down the line, then Bartlett sped after with the eagle's beak handle of his cane hooked onto the wire.

On the ceremonial platform, Don Rodrigo Gongoro and his fellow high priests stumbled blindly about, faring no better than their brethren crowded to all sides. But Declan mac Coul—or the froggish monster that had once been Declan—stood calmly, blinking the lids of its bulbous red eyes as if to clear them. There was no telling how long the flash grenades' effect would last.

And though the ritual was interrupted, the hole in the middle of the lake was still growing.

Doc Wilde shouted, and they charged up the stairs into hopeless battle.

FIFTY-FIVE

The flash blinded many of Frogon's mortal eyes, but not those of frog creatures outside the temple and certainly not Frogon's Everseeing Forever Eyes with which It watched Eternity. To those, the flash was like a star exploding in a far galaxy—minuscule.

Still, for the moment Frogon was blinded to what was happening in the temple. And It knew who was responsible. The big mammal and his minions.

Their destruction was overdue.

It would correct that problem now.

The key had turned, the darkness was opening, and It felt Its power grow in that other world, our world. Soon It would taste our universe.

For now, It washed the pain of bright light from Its army's seared eyes and ordered Its thousands to kill the mammals that had infested Its temple.

FIFTY-SIX

When sight returned to the eyes of Frogon's army, the tumult of panicked cries fell instantly to silence, and thousands of bulging eyes turned and stared at the humans charging the ceremonial platform.

As Doc Wilde reached the top, the Declan monstrosity pounced, its bulk slamming into him, nearly knocking him back. Its mouth gaping, needle teeth clashed by his face. Only through sheer strength and knowledge of anatomical physics did Doc manage to keep his feet, his mighty arms straining to keep the sharklike maw at bay.

Grandpa Wilde, Phineas Bartlett, and Carlos Gongoro found themselves fighting the three Leap One high priests, scrambling madly not to be toppled over the edge into the growing mouth of Frogon's dark portal.

Don Rodrigo Gongoro hurried toward one of the other stairways. Brian managed to slip through the fray and sprinted after him. The boy was fast, and Don Rodrigo was trying to run in robes, so Brian quickly crashed him to the stone platform with a tackle worthy of a football star.

As all this occurred, Leap Ones swarmed the four stairways, their dark elder god driving them to destroy the Wildes and their companions.

Doc grappled with the Declan beast even as a Leap One crashed onto his back, its claws raking his shoulders as another grabbed his legs—

Grandpa knocked out the high priest he fought with a single mighty punch, while Phineas Bartlett ran another through with his sword. Then they both found themselves battling the tangled mass of swarming Leap Ones, **PUNCHING,** *KICKING,* **DODGING, THROWING,** *JABBING, SLASHING*—

Carlos Gongoro was thrown to the platform by the high priest he fought, then was covered in hopping, clawing, biting shapes—

Don Rodrigo rolled on top of Brian, holding the boy down with his superior weight even as the slapping clawed feet of Leap Ones covered the stone surface around them—

Our heroes were awash in a sea of carnage, outnumbered six hundred or more to one, fighting desperately for life as the portal spread open below.

FIFTY-SEVEN

The battle was unwinnable, even for the Wildes. The slime-skinned army was too numerous, too fierce, and at any moment the hole into the dark matter universe would open wide enough for Frogon to get a grip on our world. When that happened, it'd all be over.

Yet the Wildes fought on.

Brian struggled against Don Rodrigo, who, while still seemingly human, possessed all the strength, speed, and ferocity of any Leap One. Were it not for Brian's whiplash reflexes and expert *taijutsu*, which allowed him to use the villain's force against him, it would have been a short fight indeed.

Grandpa Wilde whirled inside an endless cluster of frog-men, his hands and feet like lightning, smashing into Leap Ones, whipping their battered forms away, sending many of them plummeting off the platform into the dark and hungry mouth that led to the infinite belly of their dark and hungry god.

Phineas Bartlett jabbed and slashed with his cane but

was so swiftly crowded by the clawing Leap Ones that he had no room to use it and resorted to his own martial arts skills (which, with Doc as his *sensei*, were excellent).

Doc Wilde focused on Declan, who was far stronger and far more dangerous than the Leap Ones hanging off Doc's back trying to get a grip on his limbs.

Carlos Gongoro wasn't doing well at all. He was no warrior and fell to the Leap Ones immediately. All that saved him was the psychic resonance he shared with the Leap Ones: sensing kinship, they'd grab him, then let go. But for each that let go, another would grab. Soon he simply rolled into a tight ball, buffeted at all sides by flipper feet.

Brian wriggled free of Don Rodrigo's clutches, striking swiftly at pressure points on the *caudillo*'s torso and neck. Don Rodrigo thrashed in pain long enough for Brian to shove him away. The boy rolled to his feet, using his agility and small size to dodge around the legs and slashing swipes of the mobbing Leap Ones. He had to reach his dad and help with Declan; if they had any chance at all, it would somehow be in that fight.

Doc was having difficulty. The beast previously known as Declan was incredibly strong and seemed to want nothing more than to bite his head off. Doc, however, was trying his best *not* to hurt Declan, which put him at a big disadvantage. The Leap Ones at his sides and back weren't helping matters.

So, engaged in a battle of raw strength with the Declan monster, Doc Wilde deftly maneuvered to evade the man-frogs harrying him. Unfortunately, this brought him to the very edge of the platform, the drop into Frogon's portal at his heels. Then, leaning back to escape a gnash of Declan's needle teeth,

DOC FELL.

FIFTY-EIGHT

The Declan monster roared in triumph, but its brutish voice choked off as the creature realized Doc still held its right wrist and had pulled it over the edge with him.

Together, they fell. The emerald frog blazed bright. The portal gaped wider, seeming to breathe a hot, damp breath.

As they dropped past the stone ledge of the platform, the Declan monster lashed out with its free arm. Its claws sank into the rough edge of the platform, slicing slivers of stone as it tightened its grip, stopping its fall. It hung by that arm, its long, lean froggy muscles straining.

Beneath it, Doc Wilde swung with both powerful hands clasped around its slimy wrist.

Something moved in the dark depths below. Something sinuous. Something excited.

Above, Brian had managed to get close enough to his father and the transmogrified Declan to see them topple off the platform.

"DAD!"

Brian screamed, scrambling to the edge.

Looking down, he saw them hanging. All there was between his dad and otherworldly doom was an uncertain grasp on slippery skin.

The Declan monster heard him and looked up. It roared, its needle-toothed maw like a monstrous Venus flytrap, wide enough for Brian's head. The emerald frog blazed so brightly it hurt the boy's eyes. Then Brian caught a glimpse of movement below, in the depths of the portal. Something shot from the darkness, long and snaking.

A tentacle.

No . . .

A TONGUE.

It struck Doc and wrapped around his legs. It *pulled*.

Doc's fingers started to slip. Brian couldn't reach him in time, so he did the only thing he could think of.

He grabbed the edge of the platform and dropped, his legs swinging toward the Declan monster's mouth.

The teeth crashed together, spraying spit, but Brian managed to twist just outside the biting jaws.

The emerald frog flashed like an angry supernova as Brian kicked it as hard as he could.

The ancient carving lost its grip on the Declan monster's head and fell. Past the hanging form of its host, past the teeth-gritting Doc Wilde, down, down, down into the portal, into darkness, where it shone like a bright green star as it sank away to a different infinity.

An eerie wail arose from the army of Leap Ones: the angry voice of Frogon shrieking through thousands of throats.

The fighting stopped. The Leap Ones reeled as the sudden power of their deity's thoughts shattered their own like glass.

Don Rodrigo Gongoro felt the storm of rage as strongly as any of the fully transformed Leap Ones. He rocked blindly in place and a Leap One stumbled into him, knocking him from the platform. Don Rodrigo plummeted headfirst into endless communion with his god. It was not as joyful an experience as he might have imagined.

The Declan beast roared. Shaken by the psychic blast, it lost its grip on the platform and fell. Brian hung desperately on to the ledge above, screaming as he watched his dad fall with it.

Just as Doc and the Declan monster disappeared, the portal's sides crashed together in a great watery boom and it was gone.

A mighty reverberation rattled through the stone of the temple, indeed through the whole mountain and the territory around it that had belonged to Frogon. Stalactites fell like spears from the ceiling. Cracks zagged the floor and walls.

The Leap Ones fell to the ground as one, bulging eyes rolling back in their heads, comatose from brain shock.

The same thing happened to all the froggy things living in the mountain and the surrounding jungle.

Phineas Bartlett and Grandpa Wilde each reached down to take one of Brian's hands and pulled him onto the platform. They stared in shock at the churning water below.

"Did . . . did your father fall in the portal?" Grandpa Wilde asked in the most uncertain voice Brian had ever heard from him.

"Yes," Brian said, clutching his grandfather in a tight embrace.

FIFTY-NINE

They had to get out of the mountain. The deep reverberation that swept through it as the portal closed had not ceased. Indeed, it had deepened into an actual quake. Great chunks of jagged volcanic stone calved from the walls and ceiling to crash like thunder into the stone or water below.

One of the four stairways supporting the ceremonial platform rattled into boulders that splashed heavily into the lake.

"I RECOMMEND WE DECAMP!" Phineas Bartlett shouted over the ambient roar.

"I'M NOT LEAVING WITHOUT DAD!" Brian shouted back. He stood at the edge, staring down at the turbulent waters. His guts were in knots over the loss of his sister, the loss of his father . . .

Grandpa Wilde put a strong hand on his shoulder. He spoke in his deep, commanding voice, not needing to shout for Brian to hear. "Of course not. But let's get off this platform."

Brian nodded just as a big chunk of the platform broke off. They scrambled over the flopping Leap Ones scattered everywhere. Carlos Gongoro was in the same shock as the fully formed man-frogs; Grandpa scooped him up into his arms like a child and followed Brian and Bartlett down a cracking staircase. Just as they reached the bottom, a mammoth boulder fell and smashed the stairs to gravel.

Brian stared at the churning surface of the lake. Tears ran down his face. Then he saw motion, something in the water.

"DAD!" he shouted. *"DAD!"*

Out of churning chaos swam Doc Wilde. He kicked toward shore on his back, the Declan monster clasped to his chest. As he reached the lake's edge, Grandpa and Bartlett helped him hoist the demonic amphibian out of the water. It lay senseless on the stone, in no way looking as if it had once been a man.

Doc vaulted onto the shore and Brian jumped into his arms. "Dad," he whispered, against the sound of a mountain falling apart. But Doc, with his astonishingly tuned ears, heard him. He held his son tightly to his chest.

"WE THOUGHT YOU'D FALLEN INTO FRO-GON'S MOUTH!" Bartlett shouted.

"If it had stayed open another half instant, we would have," Doc said loudly. "I think it's time we left."

He set Brian down and lifted the Declan monster's great weight into a fireman's carry. Then he looked at his own father.

"Any ideas?" he asked.

Grandpa Wilde shook his head. "Only to move," he said.

So they moved, running toward one of the many passages that opened into the cavernous temple. They knew their chances of escape were slim. The mountain was collapsing. Carlos, the only one among them familiar enough with the lake's dark currents to lead them out, was still comatose like the army of Leap Ones. And even had he been awake to guide them, they probably wouldn't have made it in time, having to drag Declan's amphibious bulk through underwater tunnels.

As if to emphasize the hopelessness of their situation, before they could reach it, the passage they were racing for caved in with a bone-rattling crash.

SIXTY

They raced toward another passage, hoping it would lead to a way out. The entire network of caves could smash down at any moment, and they had no idea how to escape.

Then the sharply tuned ears of the three Wildes caught a faint, high sound from somewhere behind them: a whistle. "Hold!" Doc ordered; they stopped and turned to see if it was what they hoped it was.

It was. Their hearts surged as they saw Wren running toward them, zigzagging and hopping among the fallen Leap Ones.

"DAD!"

They rushed to meet her. Brian swept her into a hug that lifted his little sis off her feet, then Doc crouched,

Declan still on his shoulder, and hugged her with one arm and a kiss.

The overwhelming relief and delight they all felt was only slightly marred by their dire circumstances.

"Wren, come on!" Brian yelled. "We're looking for a way out!"

She smiled brilliantly. "I *know* a way out! Follow me!"

Wren led them out of the temple to one of the moss-carpeted antechambers at its edges. She stepped to a recessed corner and lifted a patch of moss like a trapdoor. Beneath, a small, slick tunnel vanished into the stone at an angle.

"There are little handholds in the sides you can climb," Wren told them. "But going down, you can slide!"

She slipped into it feetfirst and plunged out of sight.

Doc turned to Brian. "You next. We'll slide Declan and Carlos down after you."

Brian went, finding himself swooshing through twisty darkness. It reminded him very much of the slides in the walls at home. He smiled, enjoying it in spite of the current danger. At the bottom, he slid smoothly onto more thick moss. He stood, joining Wren off to the side, activating his light stick so they could see.

When Declan and Carlos slid out, the kids pulled them out of the way of the conscious adults who followed.

Once Wren discovered how to get out of the small caves into the big ones, finding the rest of the crew had followed fortuitously: hearing the shriek of thousands of Leap Ones, she peeked from the antechamber into the temple just as all the man-frogs collapsed and the mountain started falling apart. She saw her family and the others near the platform and ran to catch up as quickly as she could through the flopping Leap Ones and falling stone.

Given a light stick, she now led them through a cave in which they could walk, though Doc and Grandpa had to hunch a bit to keep from grazing the ceiling. They went fast, because even here rock was starting to crack around them.

"TA DA!" she shouted as they reached her most important discovery: a swift-moving subterranean river. About a hundred feet down its course, a tunnel mouth opened into sunlight.

"I already checked it out!" Wren said. "Come on!"

She dove in the river, laughing as it swept her away.

The others jumped in and let the rushing current carry them. Doc and Grandpa held on to Declan and

Carlos, making sure their heads stayed above water as they went.

At the tunnel's end, the river poured them over a smooth ledge, and they were falling, down, down, the water a crashing shower around them, down, to an abrupt splash into a deep pool fifty feet below.

It would be a three-week trek back to Verde Grande, where they'd be welcomed warmly with many smiles and lots of delicious spicy food by Carlos Gongoro's family, who'd known nothing of Carlos's uncle's treachery against all of creation. Declan mac Coul would revert to his human self almost as quickly as he'd turned monster. And Grandma Pat would join them there for the best family vacation they'd had in years. But that was the future.

Now they swam to the jungly shore. There they laughed and shouted in joy, Doc Wilde holding his kids in his arms and spinning, spinning, a spiral dance of impossible victory and the deepest-possible love.